The Calling

ILLINOIS SHORT FICTION

Crossings by Stephen Minot
A Season for Unnatural Causes by Philip F. O'Connor
Curving Road by John Stewart
Such Waltzing Was Not Easy by Gordon Weaver

Rolling All the Time by James Ballard
Love in the Winter by Daniel Curley
To Byzantium by Andrew Fetler
Small Moments by Nancy Huddleston Packer

One More River by Lester Goldberg
The Tennis Player by Kent Nelson
A Horse of Another Color by Carolyn Osborn
The Pleasures of Manhood by Robley Wilson, Jr.

The New World by Russell Banks
The Actes and Monuments by John William Corrington
Virginia Reels by William Hoffman
Up Where I Used to Live by Max Schott

The Return of Service by Jonathan Baumbach
On the Edge of the Desert by Gladys Swan
Surviving Adverse Seasons by Barry Targan
The Gasoline Wars by Jean Thompson

Desirable Aliens by John Bovey
Naming Things by H. E. Francis
Transports and Disgraces by Robert Henson
The Calling by Mary Gray Hughes

THE CALLING

Stories by Mary Gray Hughes

UNIVERSITY OF ILLINOIS PRESS

Urbana   Chicago   London

© 1980 by Mary Gray Hughes
Manufactured in the United States of America
81 82 83 84 85 P 6 5 4 3 2

"The Foreigner in the Blood," *Esquire,* February, 1968; *Best American Short Stories* (Houghton Mifflin, 1969)

"Neil," *Southwest Review,* Spring, 1977

"A Lift," *Bicentennial Collection of Texas Short Stories,* ed. James White (Texas Center for Writers Press, 1974)

"Luz," *Southwest Review,* Autumn, 1979

"The Calling," *Antioch Review,* vol. 32, no. 4, 1973

"Beginnings," *New and Experimental Literature,* ed. James White (Texas Center for Writers Press, 1975)

"Consider the Lily," *The Thousand Springs* (Puckerbrush Press, 1971)

"The Thousand Springs," *The Thousand Springs* (Puckerbrush Press, 1971); *Vision,* February, 1979

"The Valley of Zibelu," *Re: Arts & Letters,* Spring, 1971

"The Rock Garden," *Southwest Review,* Spring, 1973

"The Judge," *Atlantic Monthly,* November, 1971; *Best American Short Stories* (Houghton Mifflin, 1972)

Library of Congress Cataloging in Publication Data

Hughes, Mary Gray.
  The calling.
  (Illinois short fiction)
  CONTENTS: The foreigner in the blood.—Neil.—A lift. [etc.]
  I. Title.
PS3558.U375C3   813'.54   80-20981
ISBN   0-252-00842-1 (cloth)
ISBN   0-252-00843-X (paper)

ACKNOWLEDGMENTS

The author would like to thank the National Endowment for the Arts for a Fellowship.

Also Puckerbrush Press for important initial encouragement.

Special thanks to Ardyth Bradley and Charis Elizabeth Hughes for discussions about Alexander's words.

Contents

The Foreigner in the Blood	1
Neil	20
A Lift	39
Luz	52
The Calling	65
Beginnings	78
Consider the Lily	81
The Thousand Springs	100
The Valley of Zibelu	107
The Rock Garden	116
The Judge	126

The Foreigner in the Blood

The daughter of Leon Esteban, yes *the* Leon Esteban, committed him to a private sanatorium for elderly incompetents in July. She, Clara Rasmussen, for that was the name of the man she had married and was the name she used even professionally, signed the committing forms as a member of his family and his potential guardian, and two other doctors signed the psychiatric reports required by the law, a model law, too, which Esteban himself had drawn up for the state years ago. It was all done "according to Esteban," as his colleagues used to joke. And indeed the precipitating incident, the immediate cause of his committal, made a case as classic as any of those in his textbooks.

"Who is that strange man in my house?" he had said over the phone to his secretary and assistant. "I tell you there is a stranger in the house," and the *s*'s of his speech hissed heavily, as they did more and more the last few years. The secretary at once asked what he meant and what was he talking about, and as she began asking questions it seemed there was only some misunderstanding or other, and he said it was all quite all right and that he was on his way up to bed. She told him he had been working too hard, which was true. Two nights later he called her again, waking her from a deep sleep. "I tell you there is a strange man in my house. Who is he? What is he doing here?" By the time she was awake enough to begin talking to him and questioning him, the matter seemed again of no importance. Some shadows he had seen. In the morning she did not mention it, and neither did he. It was not until the third time he called her, in the afternoon this time, crying out, "Who is this man? I am afraid, understand? Afraid. There is a strange man here in the hall beside me," that she remembered the phone was in front of the large hall mirror, and that it was himself he saw.

She had gone at once to his home, and she had stayed with him, without protest from him either, until Clara could cancel her appointments and get a plane out from New York.

Esteban's doctor agreed Esteban must have more care now than in the past. A little more care in circumstances somewhat different, somewhat more careful of him, and he could continue his life much as before. It was decided he would be best off in some good private home. He could continue his work there and everything would be made easier for him. Many arrangements had to be made, and both women were enormously busy. Any number of homes and special hospitals for the old or sick had to be investigated and one selected. Esteban's books, papers, and notebooks had to be sorted, since he could not take them all with him. And there were the legal papers. They worked night after night to get it all done. Esteban worked with them, and seemed tactfully grateful for their help.

He said so, sometimes. Then again, he would be quite different.

"You enjoy it too much," he said to them. "You, you women. Interviewing hospitals. Signing papers. You love it."

"Now, now, you know you don't mean that," his secretary said, not so much as lifting her head from the drawer where she was going through notes of his early cases and throwing out duplicates. But Clara Rasmussen looked hard at him, her father, this clever man. How much in fact was he failing? How much of that was the querulousness of age, and how much was sheer malice, the irresistible dig? He'd always loved to tease her by making fun of her seriousness, her conscientiousness, her hard work. It was only by this she had got ahead. She hadn't his brilliance. She knew she was a drudge, but she was competent. She had published. Little Earnesta, he called her. He had done it pleasantly enough, but she had winced. How much of what he said now was intended? Did he really think she enjoyed committing him? As she stared at him, his long dark face split open like an apple with a white grin.

"Well, little Clahra," he said, for so the name came out on his foreign tongue. "Well? You were always the one who liked measurements, no? Have you decided? Am I 100 percent certifiable? Or 99 percent? Or maybe . . . 63 percent?"

"Papa, stop it. Tell me which of these books you want to take. Pick out which ones you want. If you change your mind, I can always bring you different ones later."

"Later? What do you mean later? How long are you staying?" So hopefully, so anxiously and hopefully, completely different from his manner the second before.

On the spur of the moment, because of his face, she said, "All summer. Peter can come out and spend his vacation here, and I'll stay here all summer."

And Esteban spun away from her and half-ran out of the room.

"He's so up and down, so all mixed up," Clara said to the secretary.

"Now, now, never mind. He's old, you know, Clara," the secretary answered.

When the time came Clara drove Esteban to the Home in his car, which was piled with books and files and, in suitcases and on hangers, quantities of Esteban's lovely clothes. He was to have a corner room. Clara had seen to that. And she had replaced the dark green, flowered curtains with plain good white ones. She had not been able to get them to repaint the light green walls.

From a few steps into the center of the room Esteban stood surveying it. In his linen suit, among the institutional furniture, surrounded by short-sleeved attendants bringing in his belongings, he was completely out of place.

"Well, do you like it? Is it all right, do you think? Papa?" Master, she might have called him. Teacher. A giant in the field. He had known Freud. He would certainly see the farce in it, that he should be here, in the little corner room with good curtains at the two windows (special rate for two windows) and not enough bookshelf room to hold even the books that he, Esteban himself, had written.

"I couldn't get them to paint the walls yet," Clara said. "But I could have a painter come in and do it. I'm sure of that."

"You can't change everything. See, am I not being good?"

"Papa, stop that. Stop. If you don't like it, I'll take you right out. You know that. We can make other arrangements . . . oh yes we can, don't look like that. You could stay at home, if you want. I could shift my practice here."

"And Peter? Nonsense, Clahra. No such thing. Some things now I must give up. It must be. Let strangers deprive me of things, that is better than your doing it. Now, send Alice soon to help me with the typing. And you must again be my assistant until I am settled. It will be fine, yes? Only, you are sure they understand about all this, and you and Alice are to come and go as we please? Good. One thing, tell that little man, the fat one, what's his name?"

"Hoffman."

"Tell him to stay away from me. I don't like that little fat man."

"But he's the director," she said. "He's not really fat. He's quite good. Really. He told me they were honored to have you here. He knows your work."

"Ha ha ha. Honored, fine. Honored. I know that type. He's my jailer, Clahra. Only I don't have to like him. Remember? All the best analysts say that. I don't have to like anyone for such a thing."

It turned out to be unfortunate about the director's name. Esteban said he could never remember it, or never remember it correctly. He delighted in making variations on it: Hausmann, Hausfrau, Hauptman, Helpman. Even Faust. But occasionally he was genuinely not able to remember the name, and his sharp bright face would bunch up with the effort, as if something were jammed, and in an instant he would grow old, ancient, before one's eyes. Yet other than this, he accepted it remarkably well, Clara thought. He worked long hours in his corner room, dictating from his old notes and correcting the drafts of typescripts. He called for one volume after another to check references or reread papers. The finished papers piled up on his desk with Clara working hard as his assistant, as she had years ago, but with a great difference now. She had her own career and her own life, which had to be kept up as well.

She established her family in Esteban's home and took over the few patients he still had. She commuted by jet to New York each week to take care of her own practice. She had never had such a busy, expensive life of such sophistication. She loved the jets and all the rituals of flying: the care, the cocktails, even the food. She had never felt so solemnly adult, so important. And everywhere people in her profession knew of her father's trouble and how she was managing it. Everyone asked about him, and as in her early days as a practicing analyst she had amused psychiatrists with stories of the great Esteban's problems with American pronunciation, or American slang, now she told over and over the classic story of how he had not recognized himself in the mirror, and so had been committed. It was a remarkable story. Whenever she told it there would be a pause of silence afterward. Then she would be asked how he was doing, and she would tell of his fights with Hope-man. It went over very well. Too well. She found it hard to stop. One rainy wretched day she realized she had twice, in different groups at a New York cocktail party, brought the conversation around so that she could tell her story on Esteban. And that's what it had become—a story on Esteban.

"Enjoying it too much?" Esteban had said. Was she? Probably. Yes, probably, damn him. He knew. Hadn't he written, in a famous paper, *If only the young would take as their revenge the damage time will inflict upon their parents, they would not need to indulge in those actions or thoughts which sully their minds with guilt.* The word "sully" had been particularly admired in analytic circles. When Clara first read the paper (she was the most talented of his protégés at this time, and his "closest critic," it amused him to say) she said only, assuming as she often did the right to a much greater understanding of the United States than he, a foreigner, could have, "Papa, you never will understand Americans must do something themselves. They don't get satisfaction from anything that just happens. They are first and always doers."

He had laughed. So many American words, like "doer," amused him. But he had not changed anything in the paper. Sometimes he made changes when she had suggestions, most often he did not. And everything he did was successful anyway. Everyone admired him.

Except at the Home. At the Home, Esteban was beginning to have difficulties. When she visited him and found him working, as she always did, and worked with him, he seemed as active and agile, as excited about his work and as alert, or almost as alert, as ever. It seemed then only because of some matter of strange convenience that he should be living in a tiny corner room in a home for the senile and deranged. Yet the staff told her other things: that he could never remember how to get to the dining hall and an attendant had to be sent for him. That he didn't want to change out of his clothes at night and get into his pajamas. That he threw things on the floor. Petty little things. Institutional offenses. Half deliberate, she suspected, done with the malice of the angry but sane. He had always liked jokes. If these were stranger ones, pettier ones, who could blame him? All the silly rules of the place, all the dull people staffing it. He was bound to hit back. *She* had no trouble with him.

Yet one of their complaints about him, she could see, did give them real trouble. That was his dislike for the director. It was amusing to call Hoffman names behind his back, but lately Esteban had begun doing it openly, and often before other patients. It disturbed them, the director said. "Half-man," Esteban yelled at him, right in the common living room. And when Hoffman went on by, Esteban had spat after him onto the floor. It was foolish, childish, Clara told Esteban. He didn't need to do that sort of thing. He could avoid Hoffman if he wished.

"Don't worry," Esteban said. "You always worry too much. Bring me some oranges, Clahra. We never get any decent fruit in this place. Bring me some Spanish oranges I can suck on," and he held his hand up before his face with the fingers curved around an imaginary orange, "something I can get some juice out of."

Blood oranges, he meant. She bought a net sack of them at the market south of town.

"What a gloomy name for an orange," her husband said. "Who wants to eat blood? It's that old macabre Latin sense."

"He's not Latin. He's Spanish," Clara said, but she wasn't paying much attention. She was packing food in a small kit. Her husband watched with a bland weighing eye and from time to time would reach in and rearrange a box or the thermos so that it would fit compactly. He was much better at this sort of thing than she was. He often came along, chatting with her and helping when she tidied the house or put away the clothes because he was the better at it and because it was a pleasant time to talk. He was a geologist who ran a small firm that did consulting for oil companies. He knew nothing of analysis. Her work was always an amazement to him, as was his to her, and they constantly brought each other gifts of novel information and delighting, fresh ideas, for their minds, like most of the hours of their days, ran along quite separately but side by side, with hundreds of ties across. Her father, however, was not one of them and, with Esteban, Rasmussen shared nothing.

"I'm taking him out for a drive," she said. "I hate seeing him cooped up in that place all the time. It must get on him. It gets on me. All those dreadful people, sick and old or addled. And the dim-witted staff. I can't work with him there anymore." She could not focus on him, she meant. She felt she could not seem to see him, could not get through to him to do any real work, anything that was not the simplest routine.

"Well, be careful."

"Don't be silly, he's my father," she said.

Esteban was not expecting her. He was standing by one of the two windows. He was without jacket and tie, and he was leaning forward with his hand touching the screen. It was a heavy one of the sort that could not be opened from the inside. She was sure it had not been there when she had taken the room.

"Papa," she said. He seemed disconcerted by her being there. "I came early," she said. "It's Sunday . . . and I'm quite early."

"Yes. All right. I was thinking. I have been thinking of the meanings of the disrobing of Christ."

"Good heavens."

"Have you thought about it? Think about it."

"Okay, if I have to. But later. I've got a surprise."

He brightened. "Oh, listen, Clahra, I have a surprise. I, too. Such a funny thing this morning. Let me tell you. It's really very funny. Hoffman came to see me. He came in," and he began to mimic Hoffman, for despite his accent and his sharp Spanish face, he had a gift for mimicry and could catch the voice and look of his victim. "'Ah, ah, ah now, good morning now, ah now, Dr. Esteban.' He's never learned I am not an M.D. We weren't in those days," he said. Then he switched roles again, drooping his shoulders and pushing out a nonexistent tummy. "'My dear Dr. Esteban, I wonder if, ah now, you couldn't help me out.' You see the direction, Clahra? I am to help the big director. Oh I am to be flattered." She began to smile. What a fool Hoffman was to think he could try anything like that with Papa. "So I, I keep a straight still face, very still . . . like in a session, understand? 'I'm in need of some references for a paper,' he says. 'I've been doing a little, ah now, ah now, work, ha ha.' He can't even come out and say the word decently. He doesn't know the meaning of the word and knows it, so he gives a little apologetic laugh, 'ha ha,' when he says 'work.' 'I've been doing a little work, ha ha,' he says, 'with chlorpromazine among our more, um, ah now, elderly patients here.' All the time I am blank, a blank face, but just beginning to let it go a little stupid, a little slack and stupid. Not too much. 'My assistant seems to remember some work along these lines done in a veterans' hospital. We thought perhaps you, ah now, perhaps you might remember. . . .' He had even set me such a simple task, you see, so I could give the answer and get the prize. That paper by Belanjian and Emerson. Oh just the right degree of difficulty. But recent, to test how much I remembered recently."

"Oh Papa, really you can't be sure of that!" But she could not help laughing too. He was impossible, her father.

"On he goes," Esteban said, "giving me all the clues, more and more, suggesting a name, even their names, and I get a bit stupider, a bit slacker. He calls the names out, and I stare. And oh he is happy. He begins to smile. I am foolish, he thinks. I am foolish and he is quite sure. He smiles, you see, he thinks he knows just how the mind is gone. He is happy, he is certain. He is ready to go. I let him take a step, another, then I straighten my face, stern, stern, the look of a father to an errant son, indignation, the hard stare, and I say, in good medical Latin, the words for gullible fool, sucker you know. And I spell it for him. Don't worry, he'll look it up. I know the type. Ah it was perfect, perfect. He doesn't know, you see, how much I meant it, how much of what he was saying I comprehended totally.

He doesn't know if I am foolish or joking or lucky. All his certainty gone. Ha ha ha ha. Hoffnut."

"Oh Papa!" But she was laughing with him and was elated, too. "You're impossible," she said. But what did Hoffman expect, that Esteban was some ordinary slobbering old man?

"We'll celebrate," she said. "I've been tied to a desk all week and I want to get out. Let's have a picnic snack, out at Mt. Schyler Park like we used to do. Get some air. Do us both good. We can take something to work on and work with clear heads. Just like we used to do years ago. We can take some of the notebooks Alice has typed up. Let's take some of the early New York ones. You get them, and whatever else you want, and I'll go tell someone on the staff."

"Ask permission you mean?" Esteban said.

"Yes." She laughed, but with him. "All right, yes. From old Halfbrow." And she left the room smiling still.

But permission was not so easy to get. She did have to see Hoffman. She could not just tell a secretary. And Hoffman was against it. In his office, behind his desk, he seemed a nice, sensible, rather heavyset man trying to do his job, and some of her elation left her. He did not want Esteban to go out.

"I don't see why," she said. "How do you find him, then? Isn't he doing well? Doctor?" she added, switching sides.

"I find his condition discouraging and deteriorating, frankly, Doctor."

"You have to make allowance that he has always been, well, eccentric. He's always liked his little jokes."

He waved all that aside. There went Leon Esteban, his wave said. "No no, I'm not talking about that," he answered her. "He's showing difficult signs. We feel, we have found, that he needs very careful handling. More than I think you realize."

"What exactly do you mean?"

"A phase comes over him now and then when he is extremely excitable and frenzied. He gets difficult. I mean physically, Doctor. We have all come to recognize it. We call it his hyena phase."

She hated him. For his accuracy. It was true. She had seen it herself. She had seen it the night they were boxing his notebooks and he had said she enjoyed it too much. Yes, she had. She had seen it, but she had not named it and so had forgotten it. Now she would always know it. No, it was too horrible. She refused.

"I don't agree," she said. "I don't agree at all. You've forgotten how depressing this place can be to someone used to a quite different life. You don't realize how confining, I mean intellectually of course, it can be for a man like my father. He needs to get out more. To be free of nurses and staff and administrators. I think he should be taken out much more. I feel I have been very remiss in not having done so before. I am sure it will help him."

"Where do you want to take him?"

"I thought I'd start with a little picnic in Mt. Schyler Park. We used to go there frequently."

"You want to take him yourself? Alone?"

"Of course. Oh, Dr. Hoffman, he's a tiny old man. Come now."

"I am against it. Absolutely against it. But I don't feel I can refuse you if you are set on it. I do insist, however, you take my car. Yes, I insist. It's equipped for such purposes. It has two doors only, and both have special locks which are difficult to open and which are set down low. I'll show you how they work. I insist that you take it."

"What took you so long?" Esteban asked when she got back. He was fully dressed, standing, and plainly fretful from waiting.

"Silliness," she said.

"They didn't want to let me go, did they?"

"It just took time to get some arrangements made. You know how these places are, Papa. They excrete red tape."

He became more relaxed as they left the white stucco building. She had been right to take him out. She was sure. She kept talking as they walked to the car and got in, and apparently he attached no importance to the change of car. He rode beside her with obvious and excited pleasure. And he looked so nice. She felt ashamed that she had not taken him out long before.

They reached the park after about a half-hour drive and she paid the fifty-cent entrance fee and started up the low slopes of the mountain. Clara intended to stop at one of the lower picnic areas, but

The Foreigner in the Blood

Esteban asked her to go higher. He wanted to see the scrub cedar where it was thick and smelled good, he said, up near the top.

"All right," she said, and turned the car and began the winding drive upward.

"Go way up," he said. "That's right, to the little parking place just below the peak. It's not a steep drive, Fidélia."

She jumped, startled, but his face was blank, unnoticing. He gave no sign of the slip. There was nothing sharp, nothing crafty in his face.

At the topmost picnic area, where it was rocky and there was dense scrub cedar, she drove the car gently off the highway, bumping slowly over the rough half-rock half-grass terrain, and stopped as close as she could get beside one of the picnic tables.

"Hmmm, I love the air up here," she said. "I haven't come enough. We must do this more often." She got out and began unloading the little basket of food and utensils and the notebooks and papers he had brought.

Esteban got out too, walked slowly around the open picnic area, and then wandered over to stand by one of the little green cedars, seemingly with his hands buried in it. She had taken all their things out of the car and was trying to arrange them on the table in some order, aware she was never as neat as he.

"Well," she said. "I don't know if we'll get any work done here, but it is nice. You know I came up here once on a geology field trip. That was a long time ago. We were hunting fossils. They brought us in a bus and parked it down at the first picnic area, and we had to hike up the rest of the way. You know I'm terrible at that sort of thing, and after a few hundred feet I was panting like a haying machine. At first I was one of the ones in the lead, but gradually everyone went past me. Two of the boys tried to haul me along, but finally that wouldn't do either. We'd come to find little fossil snails and sea animals. All things that could be found here because of the fault that runs this side of town. Well, I'd had it. I couldn't go a foot further, dragged or not, and I just sat down on a rock and gasped. To hell with it, I thought. I could hear them all marching along, higher and higher, and I sat on my rock gasping and staring at my feet, and right there, between my feet, were fossils." She laughed at the memory. "I found as many fossils as anyone. They went scrabbling all over the mountain, in and out among bushes, and I just sat picking up fossils from between my feet. You know, I should have brought a couple of blankets, or an air mattress. This bench is going to be hard after a while."

He was still standing almost into the branches of the cedar. Smelling it? Holding it? Good Lord, could he be urinating in it?

"Shall we have something to eat first, or do you want to go over some of these notes?"

"No, no. Fidélia," he said.

"Papa. You know I'm Clara."

He smiled at her. A sweet smile at first, but with something sly developing in it. It stayed on his face too long. And he was standing so far away from her. Halfway across the picnic area from her, and halfway behind that bush. Was he playing a game? Or what?

She sat on the bench. She opened a notebook, then another one. But she could not bring it off. She could not read them. He was watching her.

"I'm Clara," she said again.

"Don't worry," he said. "Don't worry. You were always such a worrier. You were always afraid I'd make a mistake in a paper. Change this, you'd say, change that. Look out, Papa, look out." Mimicking her voice and a little earnest nodding gesture of her head. Oh, he was good at it. "This might be wrong, Papa. Or that. You were good at finding my mistakes."

"It was how we worked," she said. "You wanted me to do it. You didn't even want me to go away to New York. Remember?"

"Remember?" he mimicked her. "No. You liked finding the mistakes. You were one for measurement, and you liked finding the mistakes." He was relishing the hurt.

"That's not so, Papa." She stood up. Instantly he was around the bush and farther away from her, with the little scrub cedar between them. He peered over the top of it at her, watching her, his eyes liquid and shining, pouring out malice from the sharp, the hyena face.

"Look, Papa," she began. Then, "Let's eat."

"Look, Papa," he said. "Let's eat."

"Stop it."

"Stop it."

She could not stand the way he looked, and took two quick steps toward him, but he flitted away, completely out of sight this time. She had lost him. She rushed, ran, to the bush, and on then to the next one. But her high heels (why had she worn them? But every time she had gone to see him, every time, she had dressed up, had dressed in heels and stockings and a pretty dress), the useless heels slid and lost traction and threw her off balance and she skittered to a stop. She could not run. She could not possibly catch him. Where was he?

"Clahra," he called.

She turned her head. He was across the picnic area. On the other side near the car. How had he got there so fast? Thank God she had automatically put the key in her pocket. From just this side of the car he was watching her.

"Professor Esteban," she said sharply.

"No no." He laughed. "No no no. I wrote that one, remember? *Systems of Approach and Treatment.* Esteban and Holloway. Page 328 of the revised edition. Ha ha ha."

"All right. Papa then. Help me, Papa." But he shook his head, threw off the plea, and watched her, waited, expectant and still.

She began walking in his general direction, but not directly toward him. Moving instead so she might be able to cut him off if he started back for the scrub cedars. She had to get him. He could so easily get hurt here. He could fall or get lost. He was a small old man, no matter his fancy clothes or his quickness. She came closer to him, but he laughed and moved back to keep a bush between them, and there he stood, poised and waiting and expectant again, watching her over the top of the bush. If she could get close enough she could reach over and grab him. The scratchy little stiff branches would give way. She could reach through them for him. Again she walked closer to him, but slowly. She was beginning to perspire. Deliberately she slowed her pace, broke it up, made it irregular, but moved closer.

"Bye bye," he said, and ducked his head, bent over, and was gone from sight. She rushed after him, quickly quickly, teetering on the high heels, trying to cut between the bushes and perhaps surprise him. Quick quick, cut him off, get him. And she slid again, stumbled, and caught herself only by grabbing a limb of one of the cedar bushes and hanging onto the green bristly thing.

"Hell," she said.

There was a noise beside her. She raised her head and just above her—he must have been standing on a rock—was Esteban. Right there, on the other side of the bush she was holding. He was delighted. Delighted. He stuck his face forward between the bushes, with his eyebrows arched and his eyes wide, in a pantomime, a child's exaggeration of surprise. "Peek-a-boo," he shouted in her face, and jerked back, doubled over, and was out of sight.

In despair and rage she crashed through the side of the bush after him and so suddenly that she saw him, stretched out her hand for him as he ran doubled over, crafty, animal-like, and she almost had hold of him, almost had him, and then her heel caught and held this time, in the scrub bush, and she was thrown forward and down with the full force of her plunge after him, and she crashed hard onto one knee, crying out.

Silence.

Then, "Oh oh oh," she said.

"Are you . . . all right?" she heard. An old man's voice. An old man's weak voice. "Clahra?"

She did not answer. No reply to this plea and pretense of sanity. Shaken, hurt, bleeding, covered with dirt, her stocking torn, trembling all over outside, she was like marble inside, cool and hard and one piece. Watching her blood ooze through the wide scrape on her knee, through her ripped stocking, coming up like red grass out of the brown torn stocking, soothing and holding her knee, rubbing the hurt, rocking back and forth and watching the blood, she knew her father was an old man deranged in his senility. Was mad. "Oh oh oh," she said, rocking her knee, holding it. "Oh oh," but saying it automatically, for inside she was still and certain and calm. From her pocket she took a Kleenex and sopped the blood, sopped and sopped it. "Oh oh oh." More blood. Oozing blood. And it was Esteban who had written, *Remember how ancient and how deep is the fear of madness, of this terrible derangement of our very selves. Illness, even death seem natural to us. Part of the life of the body. But insanity, in all forms, comes as a foreigner rising in our own blood, and is the more horrifying because of the very intimacy of its strangeness.*

Slowly she stopped the ooze of blood. Slowly her outer trembling ceased. The blood, the dirt on her, her weakness, her apparent hurt, these were her weapons now.

Slowly, slowly, with great fatigue and great difficulty, barely able to do it, she pulled herself up and moved over to sit on a rock. There she sat, hunched forward, a lump of despair and hurt and shattered strength. She did not answer his two or three callings of her name. She did not look up when he came nearer. She sat.

Slowly she reached into her pocket and brought out cigarettes. Slowly, shakily, she fished out one cigarette. Then dropped it, reached for it, couldn't lift it, and began again fumbling for another. Finally she got it out, tried to put it in her mouth, seemed unable to do so, and rested, both arms limp on her legs, head down, too weak to smoke. Again she put the cigarette in her mouth, raised her head, and began searching clumsily for a match, first in one pocket, then in another, then back to the first.

"You have a match?" she said.

"Oh yes," he said. "I am allowed the tiny sort." And he approached. Was it going to be this simple? No. From a few steps away he tossed the packet to her. But he did not step back. He stayed. She seemed hardly to notice where the matches had fallen. Then with great slowness and fatigue, she reached down, found them, dropped them, got them again. She lit one, and it went out. She lit another, it held, and with it finally she got the cigarette lit. She inhaled slowly, deeply, then let her head slump down as before. Exhausted. Helpless. The sun blazing on her.

"Want one?" she asked him, her voice dull, indifferent.

"Oh no," he said. But still he did not move away. He shifted back and forth, standing first on one small rock and then on another. More and more restless. It was no fun now. She sat. He moved back and forth, this rock, then that one, then this one, but all within a tiny space, like a butterfly. More and more quick and restless. "Oh no no," he said. "I am not allowed to smoke. You should know that. I'm surprised at you. You wouldn't really offer me a cigarette, would you? You should know better."

She poked at the dirt with one hand, paying no attention to him. She was slumped so far forward it seemed she could not even see him.

"You wouldn't really offer me one, would you? Are you hurt? Not if you can smoke. You should give it up. It's bad for you. Why don't you give it up? It poisons the entire body. You may already have cancer. Do you know that? Do you cough much? Women are susceptible to it, too. Especially women of your build. On the heavy side. You should lose some weight. I never put on weight. Smoking is bad for your eyesight, too. You have very bad eyesight, Clahra. You can't see nearly as well as I. I can see far better. I have perfect eyesight. You can't see that line of trees across the valley," he swung his arm out to point at them, "but I, I can make out what kind of trees they are and I can see, in among them, yes, I can see some, oh, some, let me see—" and in that instant she was up and had thrown herself forward and on him, arms and body spread around him like a net, springing and jumping on him all before he could no more than turn his head around toward her in surprise, and then they both went down, clumping together onto their knees with her arms wrapped around him. She had him. She had him and held him fiercely. Such a frail little old man, a thin bony little man. Yet she stood up and jerked him with her, holding and handling him more roughly, she knew, than she had to, but she was not able to stop. She turned him around and tugged down his jacket, the lovely pale linen jacket, until it was halfway down his arms, pinning them.

"Ah, Clahra," he said. "Too much. It's melodrama. Your timing was good, but don't do this, it's silly."

"Stop it. Stop that," she said. "Don't pretend you're joking. I'm not Hoffman, and you stop pretending you're playing a game. It won't do. You have to have help, Papa."

"Ha ha ha ha ha."

But she would not let herself mind. She took him to the car and put him into the back of it, and reached across the seat to fasten one lock and then through the window to lock the other door. Probably Esteban could open them. Probably he had invented the locks. But it would take him time to do it and she would be able to get back to the car before he got out. She gathered up the picnic lunch, the books and papers and shoved them into the trunk. Mustn't leave anything in the car for him to throw at her. Then she unlocked the door, got in, and settled herself behind the wheel, leaving Esteban in the back like a prisoner. It was terrible, but it was safe, and it was right. What if he had come to harm through her? What if he had been hurt because she had been stubborn and insisted he was perfectly competent. Thought he was joking! She would never have forgiven herself if some harm had come to him through her.

"I'm sorry, Papa. I have to make sure you aren't hurt. You understand that. I know you do. Papa?"

He sulked and would not answer. She turned the rear-view mirror so he could not find a place to sit where she could not see him by glancing at it.

"Who was Fidélia?" she asked.

He would not answer.

"Come on, Papa. Talk to me." But he would not. He sat in the middle of the back seat staring with venom at the back of her neck. So they rode, in silence, back to the Home.

Once there, as they drove into the parking area before the stucco building, he became more cheerful. When she helped him out of the car he asked, "Is it about five?"

"Just four-thirty," she said. She let an attendant take him to his room, and she went to sign him in.

"Have a little trouble?" Hoffman asked, distinctly pleased.

She was dirty. Her hair was down. Her knee and stocking were crusted with blood. "Yes," she said. "But it was nothing that I couldn't handle."

"All the same, you better not take him out again."

"No," she said.

She insisted on taking care of Esteban and helping him change his clothes, and she sent the male nurse out of the room. But Esteban refused to put on his pajamas and robe. "They always want me to do that, to prevent it, but I won't do it, I won't," he said. He was near bursting into tears, and here, where he was safe, among his books and papers and the books that he had written, seeing him nearly crying she lost all her inner firmness, and she let him do whatever he wished. She helped him select and put on one of his fine suits.

"Now," he said. "Do I look all right? Is it all nice?"

"You look fine, fine. But why the blue shirt with it?"

His face turned crafty and he smiled slyly at her and stroked the shirt with his fingertips.

"Wear what you want, please," she said. "Shall I tidy some of the books? Wait, where are you moving that chair? It's heavy."

"Here. Over here, with the light, in range of . . . of . . . it," and he nodded at it. The mirror, he meant. "Here in its focus," he said. "Hurry, hurry, little one, it's almost time."

"Time for what?"

He looked all around the room, first at the door and at each of the two windows, and then he said, lowering his voice and with his eyes and face hyena sharp, "Closer. Now listen," he whispered, "Fidélia." (Oh it was not her name. And it was not one of the names he had called her when she was small and her hair still fair and eyes, he said, that were green, and he would pick her up and rub his nose on her and call her his little golden penny, his little green pine tree. It was not even the name of her mother. It was not the name of anyone she knew.) "Listen, they mustn't hear. They try to stop me, but they can't. They'd find mistakes . . . ha ha ha . . . but on Sunday, and sometimes special during the week, I speak to the whole world. Me, I'm on," and he nodded at the mirror, "on TV."

Her mouth, her eyes broke wide in dismay. Oh Papa, oh dear God, oh it was so usual, it was so mundane, so unoriginal, so common, oh dear God, it was so trite.

He was watching her, greedy for her amazement, her awe.

"Well, I . . . I . . . uh, Papa, I. . . ."

"Shh, shh, quick," and he seated himself in the chair, very erect and proud and stiff, the mirror reflecting him in profile. He pulled, tugged on her arm, pulled her down saying, "You must get out of range, get out of range, yes, yes," the *s*'s hissing. "Soon it starts, soon I will be on and you can see it, yes, yes," and from the corner of his eye he watched his profile in the mirror. "Any minute now, see," he said to her. So proud. "Well? Well, little one?"

"How nice. It's nice. It's great for you," she said, for he had written, *Don't argue with the old.* "Do you like doing it?" she asked, for *Indulge the senile,* he had said in that book that was the textbook of their science. "What . . . tell me what . . . oh God, what channel are you on, Papa?" Hadn't he written, *Allow them the pleasures of their sad fantasies, for how shall it harm you?*

Oh Papa, no, you were wrong, it's not like that, it's not, it's not.

"Lower," he said. "Down lower," pulling her arm.

"Papa," she said. "Shh, shh," he hissed, still pulling on her arm. "Papa," she whispered, "Papa," and her head came to rest against his sharp and bony knee, his hard old bony knee. "Shh," he said, "shh, shh," but gently now, soothing her, petting her with his hand, stroking her hair with his hand over and over again, tenderly, automatically, abstractedly, his mind elsewhere.

Neil

He had been taking care of children younger than himself as far back as he could remember. He did not know a time when he had walked down a sidewalk and a balloon-sized head had not bobbed there beside him somewhere between his chest and belt and he had not had the feel of shorter fingers wrapped tenaciously around his own. His first and nearest sister had been born before he was two, then after had come, close on one another, his two brothers, and years later the new, healthy sister.

His mother worked. One of his aunts took care of them in her house after school, when school was in session, and now during the summer kept them at her house all day long. Lunchtimes she would lead them out onto the back porch, twelve gray painted steps above the fenced back yard where they were to play, and she would set down on the porch table a tray with lemonade in a plastic pitcher ("I know how children break things," she said) and enough bread, butter, and sugar sandwiches for the day because she had a dozen errands she had to run, she said.

"Neil'll watch after you," she said brightly. "He's big enough to do that. Aren't you, Neil?"

The brothers were already down in the shallow trench beside the porch playing in dust which was finer than flour. They made roads there and drove small toy cars and old matchboxes they pretended were more cars along their roadways. They were busy and paid no attention to their aunt.

Elena was older and heard. She came close behind Neil and slipped two fingers into the back pocket of his shorts, hitching herself to him.

"I know all about kids and what they get up to," their aunt said. "You behave, or I'll find out about it. None of your tricks, Neil, hear me? I know what boys do." Her voice was gay and glittering, like the shiny dangling earrings that quivered with her every movement as if they were tiny fishhooks glinting in the sunlight. "I know what boys do," she said. "You be good now, or I'll get you."

She went inside and locked the screen door, so they could not get into the house, then disappeared from their sight. If they had wanted, they could have listened to her high-heeled steps clipping down the hall and diminishing out the front door of her house.

Neil started across the big yard, and Elena, still attached to his shorts, tagged behind him, bumping against him when he stopped to pry a pointed stone out of his bare instep.

The yard was dusty and the grass so burnt it crinkled beneath their feet. Originally the yard had been planned for elegance, and a wrought-iron fence looped and whorled around the two longer sides and the brick wall that sealed off the back was lined with orange and grapefruit trees that were untended now, but beneath and slightly in front of them, as by a miracle, was a thick row of blooming gardenia bushes.

Neil pushed between two of the dark green bushes with Elena behind him, and the two of them settled comfortably in a hollow worn by their almost daily use. The trees would give afternoon shade, and the dense gardenia bushes were a screen through which they could watch when they wanted and yet feel hidden.

Neil stored a reserve of books, wrapped in two plastic bags, between the bushes. He brushed away the covering of leaves and dry grass. Elena watched. Close by her face was a tiny gardenia bud, shut tight as a crying baby's eye against opening and having at the base of its clamped outer leaves a faint green color. Elena popped it once with her finger.

"There's poison in gardenias," Neil told her. "Don't put that near your lips."

"Is it poison before it's open?" she asked him.

"It's more poisonous before it blooms because it's more concentrated. It's really poisonous now," he said. She looked at the hard, locked bud with satisfaction.

"Lots of flowers have poisons, don't they?" Elena asked him. "Which ones do, Neil?"

He began reciting them for her. "Oleanders do, and cherry pits, and poinsettias, and tomato leaves."

She knew them. He had said them over to her before, but she liked hearing them and he was used to her wanting to have them listed out loud again. As he was used to the paleness of her skin and the veins riding near the surface, struggling with her blood. Her heart was different, their mother had told them. That was her sickness. It squeezed too hard on her blood and that was why she did not grow bigger faster and could not get an easy breath and why she was cobweb frail. Neil could see the pulse snaking through her temple and the skin over it which was a pale, bruised color.

"What else?" she asked, because he had stopped naming them.

"Oh, castor beans, and lots of others," he said. "Elephant ears. And then there's cheeses. There's cheeses that have bugs in them you can't see except with a microscope and they can't bring them into the United States. People in other countries eat those bugs."

"Does it make them sick?" she asked.

But the brothers had begun quarreling loudly over whose turn it was to pour out lemonade and they were pulling and tugging the pitcher between them.

"Put that down!" Neil yelled. He jumped up and ran across the yard to get it before they could spill the day's lemonade. He grabbed the pitcher from them and shoved Robin, the older and larger, behind the porch table. "I'll pour it," Neil said.

"It's my turn. Give it to me, it's mine!" Robin shouted at him. Neil kept the table between them steady and poured two cups half full. Then he climbed up on the porch railing and by stretching slid the pitcher onto a high shelf, built evidently for flower pots, which the brothers, no matter what they used, could not reach.

"Don't go walking with that in your mouth, you'll poke yourself," Neil called down to Amos, the smaller brother, who was going into the trench carrying his cup between both hands and holding an old table knife between his teeth.

"He can do what he wants. He doesn't have to do what you say," Robin shouted. "You do what you want, Amos. Neil's nobody's boss." But he kept behind the table, out of Neil's reach.

Amos was sitting in the trench with concentration and cautiously beginning to pour the lemonade in a thin, yellow stream surrounding one of the cars becoming islanded in the dust.

"Hey, stupid, you're wasting it, stupid," Robin said to him.

"He doesn't like lemonade. He says it burns his mouth," Neil said. "That's why he always pours his out."

"He can pour it out if he wants," Robin said. "You're nobody's boss. Pour it out, Amos." He still wanted to argue, and yelled the sentences again, louder, because the other two were not paying any attention to him. Amos used his knife to pile up a car-wide dust bridge over the disappearing river of lemonade. Neil was walking across the yard to the gardenia bushes where Elena was.

The phone rang. They were not supposed to be able to get in the house ("I know what goes on in boys' minds," their aunt told them, gaily, the first time, locking them out on the porch), but Neil had learned long ago how to get inside. Only he never did it just to answer the phone, and the four of them stared at the house as the phone stabbed, like a dentist's drill, again and again.

Then the baby began to cry, a sudden, irate, healthy craw in the warm air.

Neil scrambled back on the porch railing, shinnied up the gutter, and climbed onto the low, sloped roof. Even though he was barefoot the corrugated tin rattled as he climbed over it to the small rear window. He kept a thin stick below the window ledge, fastened under the tin, and he used it to pry open the screen and unlatch it. He slipped in feet first, being careful not to unhinge the screen. Inside he went down the stairs into the hall where his aunt kept the baby, who was supposed to be sleeping, in a deep, blue buggy. Neil found the baby's pacifier, lost when the phone had startled it loose, and he popped it back into her mouth. She was six months old, and she was healthy. He watched her suck hard and clench her fists, suck hard and clench her fists, working herself back into sleep. Only how, Neil wondered, how was he going to get home to feed her the days his aunt might be away? This September he would be in junior high and it was too far from his aunt's house and he could not think how he was going to get there to feed her and run back in time, the way he had done from the neighborhood school in the months after she was born. He could not think how he would do it. She had fallen asleep, her fingers half-shut in fists and her lips partly open on her pacifier, and only her tongue working on it in bursts, quickly and contentedly, every few minutes.

Neil went in the kitchen and called to the others through the screen door, "Want to use the bathroom?" No one answered. He could not see Elena. She was behind the gardenia bushes. The brothers were both using old table knives to carve for themselves a new system of roads in the trench. Neil moved to the cupboard and opened it carefully, slipping his hand in protectively before he pulled back the door. One time a partly used bag of noodles had spilled out over the floor and he had had to pick them up, so he was cautious now. He dug out a congealed mound of raisins from a box and stuffed them in his pocket. And then a handful of dried apples. All to be shared with the others after careful division.

"When I grow up I'm going to be rich," Robin said as Neil counted raisins and apples. "And I'll have a truck of raisins."

"When I grow up I'm going to be rich and I'll have two trucks of raisins," Amos said.

"I'll have a whole train of raisins, and I'll have chocolates, too," Robin said. "More than you or Neil or anybody."

"I'll have two trains of raisins and chocolates and I'll have marshmallows," Amos said. It was his favorite game, and he went on playing it by himself when Robin quit. "I'll have all the trains there are and they'll be full of raisins and chocolates and marshmallows," he said. "No, I'll have the whole world full of raisins and chocolates and marshmallows. No I won't, I'll have a whole universe, no two universes full of raisins and chocolates and marshmallows," he chanted. He had crushed his apples and raisins into a sticky ball in his fist and munched on it like a winter-soft apple. Between his feet was the tunnel entrance he and Robin were making. Neil looked at it. He could have told them how to use bits of matchboxes to keep the sides from caving in, but he did not. Robin never wanted to be told how to do anything anymore.

Neil left the brothers and began walking across the yard. The grass was so browned it crackled under his feet, like thousands of tiny fried-chicken wing tips. The yard was never watered. Only the gardenia bushes were watered. Their aunt, who wore the flowers in her hair, watered them at night, and some afternoons he and Elena sat on ground that was still damp and had a comfortable pillow softness.

Neil shoved aside a branch of dense, polished green gardenia leaves and sat down beside Elena. They divided the raisins and dried apples that were theirs and picked out the bits of lint and ate the dried fruit one piece at a time, bending their heads to their scooped palms and licking for the raisin taste that grew stronger on their hands as their skin became damper and stickier.

"Wipe your hands good before we touch the books," Neil told her, but unnecessarily, for she was rubbing her palms on her shirt. Then she whipped her hands back and forth in the air. Neil took them one by one between his own and rubbed them briskly against the tingling that he knew came sometimes through her fingers.

She pulled away when she had had enough and waited for him to take out the biggest book.

It came from the public library. He had taken it out before. It was a book on the French Revolution with a huge number of illustrations, many of executions and of the guillotine, and one of Marat's death in his bath, which they always studied at length. They liked that picture especially, and the line drawing of a woman knitting at the executions and also the one of the children of Marie Antoinette. They did not care for the book as much as one on Mary Queen of Scots, with details of her beheading and their favorite picture of her little dog sniffing at the wig that had rolled free of her detached head. But the library would not let Neil have the Mary Queen of Scots book again, so he had brought the book on the French Revolution.

Sometimes, in their own home in the mornings, before the others were awake, he and Elena acted out special parts from the books, and for moments, in the flimsy light of early day, did not believe in anything except the parts they played. Elena, reciting while sitting on the bed, would be queen, courtesan, executioner, victim; and Neil would leap from bed to the top of the bureau to the chair to the bed sword-fighting, fistfighting, riding, dying, or conquering. Elena would make up new words for the characters. Neil could remember all the facts, even the little ones, he had read in history books, but she made up new words and said them in different, funny voices, and rolled the pillow into place to be a queen or soldier, and punched or shoved it as suited the role. She could always make the right endings for his stories, no matter what he started. Then when she got tired, they played quieter games or Neil read aloud to her while the brothers and the baby slept in their mother's room.

Neil had unwrapped the French Revolution book from both plastic bags.

"Turn to the Marat picture," Elena said, meaning his death. Head close to head they stared at the drawing. "How come they bathed in a horse trough?" Elena asked Neil. A question she had asked before.

"Maybe they'd broke the bathtubs," he said. It was the answer he gave each time, but it did not satisfy her.

"How can you stab in the water?" she asked.

"His top is out," Neil said.

"Was he bare? Nakeds and all?"

"Sure, what do you think, that he bathed with his clothes on?"

"I know what she says when she comes in to kill him," Elena told him. "She says, 'I will clean your soul while you wash your dirty old body.' Then she stabs him, slurp, and says, 'Now, where's the Ajax so I can scrub the tub.'"

Neil giggled delightedly, but she kept a straight face and watched him laugh.

"What's he say? When she stabs him?" Neil asked her.

"He says, 'Oh, oh,'" doing it in her squeaky-anguished voice, "'not my own blood on my clean hands. Ugh, ugh, here's the rub.'" Neil laughed so hard he was tilting into the gardenia bush. "'Farewell, dear old France, if you don't hear from me, try return mail.'"

Neil was left giggling helplessly, and she joined in covertly. When he could catch his breath he said, "Do it again?"

"Yeah, let's read it over," she said, "and you tell me again what you were reading at school about their army. Then we'll do the words for the generals."

He opened the book at the beginning of the chapter and they settled down for an afternoon of reading and playing out the parts they liked best. On some of these afternoons their aunt did not get back before their mother came for them. When their aunt did come, the two women would fight, and their mother would cry. They hated their mother then, when she cried in front of their aunt. And they hated their mother Friday afternoons, when she paid their aunt, for she cried because she did not want to pay that amount of money.

"If you had an ounce of feeling," their mother would start the argument, "just an ounce, you would do it out of family feeling."

"You try getting those kids looked after for an ounce of feeling. Try getting it done cheaper. I have to eat the same as you. I'm no gardenia. I don't bloom on sunlight and water."

"You're not good to them, you don't care. You leave them, I don't know what goes on and you don't care."

"They're never hurt or hungry. You ask them." Their aunt called each of them by name to answer. They stared at her like another species, blank and without understanding. "See, they don't say they've been hurt. They don't complain. If I didn't care for them someone would set them out like a row of turnips and they'd be beaten and mistreated. You shouldn't have had so many if you couldn't take care of them. Look at them, stairstep children with the gaps showing when he was gone because whenever he bothered to come home you could never say no. Damned deadbeat husband. Look what he gave you—some ounce of feeling, some ounce."

It was then their mother would begin to cry. Cry and pay the money and take them home.

"Neil, turn next to page one hundred and forty-three," Elena told him. It was the drawing of a woman nursing her baby at her breast while she watched for the flash of the guillotine. Neil and Elena stared at the picture.

But how was he going to get home, Neil wondered, to feed the baby once school started, how was he going to do it all the way from junior high? How was he?

There had been a time, one time, after the baby was born, that their mother had been ill and taken to the hospital. Their aunt had kept them day and night for eight days. Neil had slipped down in the nights to feed the baby because he knew his aunt would not come out of her locked bedroom to do it. Once he got the water too hot and it broke the bottle, but he and Elena had buried it the next day and no one even asked what happened to it. After that he learned to keep a hand in the pan so in the sleepy dark he could tell the temperature of the water, and if the baby was slow eating, he propped his head on the refrigerator so he would not go to sleep until she finished and he could put her down in her buggy and slip up the stairs to the room where his brothers slept in cots and Elena lay on the bed near his, lying outside the sheets breathing with light, frustrated gasps, and he would be asleep again so quickly that in the morning he could not remember how he had gotten back into bed.

They had to bathe with perfumed soap at their aunt's house and use her flowered towels and be careful among her bottles and jars and powders not to disarrange her bathroom. But she let them eat desserts first at supper and fix peanut-butter sandwiches afterward if they were still hungry. At night she told them long stories of her childhood and their mother's, but they listened as if they were being laden with heavy burdens, for they did not believe in the childhood of adults.

When their mother could have them home again she washed them all over, first the baby and the brothers, and then Elena. Neil washed himself. She gave them each a new piece of clothing and a glass of milk with Hershey's chocolate syrup. She had to sit down often, and when she did she would hold first one and then the other of them against her, and sometimes tears would strain down her face, and they did not hate her then.

But the baby was not used to and would not eat from her. Neil had to feed the baby and rock her until finally, first at night and then in the daytime, their mother could feed her. Their mother could not go back to work right away and they all stayed with her in their small house with no yard and no gardenia bushes. It made their mother weak, she said, when she dressed them and fed them and that was why she cried, she said, but sometimes she would go ahead and comb Elena's hair out in a new way for minutes on end and rock the baby extra long, and gradually she cried less. She sang to them and told them stories from the Bible or Peter Pan. The stories were too young for Neil and Elena, but even so they could not help liking being told them, and could not resist listening to their mother's voice in the once-upon-a-time lilt.

Twice in the days when their mother was home Neil went to town with boys from school on the weekends and once he went along to a movie. He told Elena what he had done with the boys and about the movie, and when they asked one Sunday their mother said yes, he could take Elena to a movie. But they had to come back because she could not walk the distance and the buses came too slowly Sundays for her to wait. Neil carried her home piggyback, her hard, fair head striking behind his ear and her voice telling him, in sharp tones of command, to run, stop, run, canter, faster, halt. They sat in the porch swing when he got back and pretended they were seeing a movie, making it up with words and descriptions of scenes. And their mother let Neil keep the money for whatever he wanted, all to himself, so that he had money that folded in his pocket, and when Elena and the brothers asked, he took it out and opened it for them and then folded it away again.

Their mother became worried overhearing Neil and Elena play and interrupted once saying, "Children, if a cry of pain is real, isn't a smile?"

Their silence, for how could they have known she would listen to them play, broke her nerve. They were in the swing outside the window where she mended. Isn't happiness, she would have cried out, real? But could not trust the sentence to her voice, fearing it would tremble, so she gathered her materials and moved away to let them play.

"Read it out loud, Neil," Elena said to him, and touched him, for he was reading to himself. "Hey, while you were reading I got a better idea. About Rizzio." Rizzio was one of their favorites. Adults were always the main sufferers in their stories, and Rizzio, the child-sized adult, was perfect. "I know we don't have the Mary Queen of Scots book," Elena said, "but we can do it from memory. I know a better way to do it."

"How?" Neil said.

"I mean, I know new words."

"Tell."

"When they've got him cornered and he begs for his life . . . you beg, Neil, you be Rizzio and beg and I'll tell you."

"'Please, mercy, kindness, justice, fairness. . . .' What else?" Neil whispered to her. His eyes were already shining.

"Squareness."

He began laughing, but went on, "'Squareness, roundness, fatness, more fairness.'"

"But they close in on him inevitably," she said in her announcing voice, "and he weeps and pleads and begs, crying 'no, no. . . .' Say that, Neil."

"'No, no,'" Neil said.

"'Forgive me, forgive me, forgive. . . .' Say it," she whispered, "and then they answer, 'Forgive, why we can't forgive because 'fore God you'll be far gone,' and they stab him dead. Now say it."

But to Neil it was irresistible and as he always did when he was laughing hard, he hid his face, burying it between his knees.

"'Forrrgive, forrr God, ye arre farrgone,'" she said in her Scots rolled *r* accent, and she could hear the muffled laughing bubbling up from where he had tucked his head, and when he did not stop she took the shaking edge of his shirt and held it between her fingers and through the cloth felt his laughing gradually cease.

Neil

He sat like a bat, his head far down between his knees and the trunk of his body suspended between his bony legs, and how, he wondered, how was he going to get home from school to feed the baby in case his aunt was not there on time?

He sat, thinking, how was he going to?

"Neil," Elena whispered to him, then urgently, "Neil, look," and she tugged his shirt with a jerk to let him know she meant it.

He raised up. Her face was close to his but turned sideways to him, and he could see in her shallow temple the thin, convoluted vein struggling with her blood. He turned his head and looked where she was staring through the gardenia bushes.

Three boys were standing by the gate. Two were Neil's age and the pudgy one of the two had been in his class. The third boy was older and taller, and it was he who stood with his knee pressing the iron gate against its chain. The brothers, watching from their trench, had become rigid with silence.

"Where's the bigger boy?" the tall boy asked. He spoke to Robin who sat open-mouthed, his hand holding a car suspended in midair. Amos, believing that if he did not look in anyone's eye he might stay invisible, stared at the gate being forced against the chain.

"His name's Neil," the pudgy boy said. "At his house a neighbor lady said he was here. Back in school he was telling all over about the wild things he can do." He bent and pulled at the sock sagging down on his sneaker.

"Yeah, where is he?" the tall boy asked again, and called out, "Neil!"

"And he kept on telling about the things he had to do all day at home," the pudgy boy said, "all that dumb taking care of little kids."

Elena had let go her hold on Neil's shirt and her hand slipped away somewhere out of his sight.

"He bragged about how dangerous and wild he is, and kept saying what he'd do and how much fun he'd have when he got away from home 'cause he isn't scared to do anything."

There was a silence, and the two brothers did not dare move.

"You here, Neil?" the pudgy boy called out. "Neil," but his voice cracked like a jagged rock and he shut his mouth.

"Hey, Neil," the tall boy picked it up.

"There he is," the other small boy said, the one who wore a faint red shirt and had a head covered with butterscotch-colored curls. "He's there in the bushes," he said.

Neil stood up at once as if he had just heard them. But he did not move closer.

"What're you doing?" the tall boy asked.

"We're getting ants," Neil said at once.

"Baby stuff," the tall boy said, making a face. "You don't want to do that. You are tall, like they said. Almost as tall as me. I'm Everett. I'm going to be in the eighth grade at the junior high. You got money? He said you showed money all around school. You still got some? I got money, see?" He produced a square of bills and spread them out to show it was true. "It's a lot," he said. "We're going to the new arcade. They got pinball machines and slot machines, and some peep shows with movies. You put a quarter in and see these movies for grown-ups and they really show it happening. You and me can get in, see, saying we're older, and then we go into the men's room and open the window and let the other guys in. Only it takes two of us 'cause one has to keep the door shut so no one busts in on us. Yesterday some man walked in and we didn't get caught, but I couldn't let the guys in. So we need two tall ones. We got money, but we need someone big as you. Want to come with us?"

Amos was picking up each of his cars and putting them close between his legs.

"Yeah, do you?" the pudgy boy repeated. He was draped, rocking, across the iron fence. His face was on the same level as his knees and the brown back of his head bobbed up and down toward Neil. "You told at school about the fantastic things you *could* do," he said, rocking away, "and how you weren't scared of a thing, 'member?"

Neil did not answer.

"That day you let me hold the money," the pudgy boy went on, still rocking, "you said you'd snitched it from your sister. You said you weren't scared and weren't going to give it back and didn't care, either, 'cause you were going to take off on your own some day, 'member?"

"I did not," Neil said.

"Sure you did, so you could have fun, that's what you said, and you'd do things none of us could even think of."

By Neil's feet Elena poked in the dirt around the base of the gardenia bush, seeming to be searching for the exact place where the stems turned into roots.

"The four of us can do wild things," the tall boy added, because Neil had not answered. "Like what you talked about. We can have fun, and we can see those peep-show movies. Want to? Come on."

"We'll take the whole afternoon," the red-shirted boy said, "and I know a store you can steal candy from, no trouble. I don't mind having candy for supper."

"We need someone your size," the tall boy said. "Come on with us, Neil. Hey?"

"Can't kneel here forever, Neil," the pudgy boy said, straightening up and looking into the yard. "Neil can't kneel forever," he sang. The three of them laughed, but the tall boy cut it short, saying, "Come on, Neil. We have to have another tall one, and it'll be fun."

"He isn't going to come," the pudgy boy said. "All that talk about the wild things he could do and he's scared to leave home."

"I gotta clean the yard," Neil said.

"Jesus, what yard?" the pudgy classmate said.

"The gardenias. Dig around the gardenias and tidy everything," Neil said. "My uncle makes me. He'll beat me if I don't."

"He's not here. He can't stop you," the pudgy boy said.

"My uncle knows everyone in town. He keeps an eye on me and knows everything I do. If I don't do what he wants, he beats on me. He means it, he uses a belt."

"What's his name?" the pudgy boy asked. "Maybe we know him."

"If you don't know his name, you can't know him," Elena said from where she squatted, digging.

"Yeah," Neil repeated. "If you don't know his name, you don't know him."

The pudgy boy threw a large clod of dirt into the street, where it landed with a soft, explosive thump. "He isn't going to come. He's chicken," he said. He tossed another clod of dirt, this one into the yard, and it landed among the roadways and cars in the trench between the brothers. Amos began to cry, silently, not looking up. Robin brushed furiously at the dirt that had fallen near him but he did not say anything.

Neil picked up the shovel that had been left in the yard near the brick wall. He went toward the three boys by the gate, dragging the shovel so it scraped across the sidewalk that ran from the gardenias to the iron gate. Originally it had been a formal sidewalk laid in tidy, carefully edged squares which over time had fragmented at the corners, leaving square after square broken into smaller pieces and crisscrossed with a variety of different patterns. The shovel made a harsh scraping as Neil dragged it, and when he reached the gate he stuck it viciously into the bare ground beside the sidewalk.

"What if you finish the yard, then could you come with us?" the tall boy said.

"He isn't going to come," the pudgy boy sang out, almost softer than they could hear.

"I won't get done, there's lots and lots to do," Neil said.

"See, I told you," the pudgy boy said.

"You don't want to stay here with little brats," the tall boy said. "We can come back later, and then you come with us."

"No," Neil said.

"What about all them things you said at school?" the pudgy boy asked him.

"Leave him alone, we need him," the tall boy said. "Suppose we come back a whole lot later, will you be done?" he asked Neil.

"I got too much to do," Neil said.

"How about tomorrow? We could start early tomorrow and then we could all take the whole day. I can get food from home and we don't have to tell anyone. We could take off on our own. How about that, Neil?"

"I could get hotdogs from home tomorrow," the red-shirted boy said.

"With four of us, we could do whatever we wanted around town," the tall boy said. "How about it, huh? Come on, Neil."

"No."

"See, I told you he was—" the pudgy one started.

"Shut up," the tall boy hissed out at him. "If he won't come, we can't all get in. Why won't you?" he asked Neil.

"I just won't, that's all," Neil said.

The three boys stayed on waiting, restless but waiting.

"There doesn't have to be a reason, but it's because I just won't," Neil said. "I won't ever."

The tall boy stepped back and let the gate swing freely in the loop of chain. "OK," he said. "OK, then. Anyway, I'll see you at school, in the junior high. I'll see you on account of like me you're one of the tall ones."

The three boys moved away down the sidewalk, following the tall one's lead. Neil jerked the shovel out of the ground where he had stabbed it and let it fall with a clang against the black wrought-iron fence. Amos quit crying and watched him, and Robin began scratching out a clean pathway for a new, imaginary road. Neil went back to the hollowed-out spot between the two gardenia bushes and sat down next to Elena, who did not speak or look at him. He watched her slyly, not wanting to fall into a straight gaze with her, but taking quick glimpses of her out of the tear-shaped corner of his eye.

She was poking in a small hole she had made with her stick. Ordinarily he would have joined her, assuming she was after an earthworm or opening the entrance to an ants' nest, but he watched her working and waited. What she was doing palled and she let go of the stick.

"Want to play?" she said.

"Yeah, sure," he said.

"Really want to?" she asked him.

"With this?" he said, taking up the book on the French Revolution.

"Doesn't matter," she said. "I've got a new idea, a whole new way to play, only better. Listen, let's make it more horrible," she said, and her gaze caught his and held like a handclasp.

"How?" he asked alertly, caught.

"Horribly horribly more horrible," she said. "Far more horrible. Listen, let's cut out their tongues. Everyone of them's tongues before they get killed."

"There'd be blood all over everywhere," Neil said, after a minute. "Spouts and streams of blood out of their mouths."

She began rocking back and forth with excitement. "Yes, yes," she said. "'Bubble bubble toil and gluggle,'" she chanted. "Don't laugh yet, Neil, hush, I'm serious. It happens to all of them, see, their tongues get cut out before they die."

"Yeah, but listen," Neil said, "does it happen to all of them?"

"Everyone. Every single one before the end. Even the ones going to have their heads chopped off."

"Only wait, wait, I don't know how they'd do it," he said. "It could be their ears or noses or something that was chopped off, but I don't know how they'd cut out people's tongues."

"No, it's got to be tongues," Elena said. "You told me once it was done sometimes, so you must remember. You remember everything."

"I don't know how they did it though."

"Well, it's got to be tongues. Mary Queen of Scots' tongue and Marie Antoinette's tongue and Rizzio's tongue and everybody's tongues. You've got to remember how they did it because it's got to be tongues."

He did not argue with her, but he did not agree with it; she knew she had not convinced him.

"See," she said, "tongues all cut out and bleeding, that's worse than ears or eyes or anything. Because then they could never say, see? They could never say anything about what had happened to them. Just 'bubble bubble toil and gluggle.' That's good, isn't it, Neil? Now don't start laughing again. That's all they could say and then anybody could do anything to them and they couldn't say."

"Do people know about it?" Neil said. "Do they know ahead of time about it and that it's going to happen to them?" He waited for her answer, and for an instant, watching him, so too did she.

Then, "Yes," she said, "they'd know. They'd get told. And their tongues would be pulled out like this," and she stretched hers out and clutching it between her fingers pulled it far down onto her chin and made a long, gurgling noise. "Like that," she said, "way out and then, wham, it's off. Then 'yugh yugh yugh,' and blood all over and they couldn't tell, couldn't say, couldn't ever say what happened, no matter what had."

"How would they get their mouths open to do it?" Neil asked. "They'd shut their jaws if they knew ahead of time."

"They must have had some tool." Elena said. "You told me once they used to do it. You must remember about it."

"No."

"It was in a big fat history book. The one with little square pictures down the sides. It was red." He shook his head. "It was a dark red with a darker red patch on the back." He shook his head again. They both sat in the soft, worn hollow, puzzling.

"I know," Elena said, "it doesn't matter 'cause they could hold their noses and they'd have to open their mouths to breathe. Wouldn't they, Neil? Isn't that right? Yes, they'd have to open their mouths to breathe. Then they'd all get their tongues cut out. And no one could get away from it, no one would get any protection. 'Yugh, yugh, yugh,' blood coming out."

"Some of them might drown in their blood," Neil said.

"Yeah, but some might not. And they could just swallow it, couldn't they, Neil? Some of them? Anyway, they could mop the blood all off them, couldn't they? They could use clothes, see, and mop all the blood so no one drowns. They could use dirty clothes, socks and anything, and mop up the blood, 'yugh yugh yugh,'" and she used her hands to show how the blood might spurt out of her mouth and be wiped up before it came over her chin and onto her chest as it flowed out of her grotesquely opened mouth, saying "'yugh yugh yugh.' See? Like that, so they couldn't drown and they couldn't say anything. They couldn't even tell lies. 'Yugh yugh yugh.' See, Neil?"

Neil saw.

"And they'd do whatever they wanted to them, wouldn't they, Neil? And they couldn't ever say. Just 'bubble bubble,'" she said in her choking voice, her special-for-strangling voice, "'toil and gluggle,' just that, but no words. No words, ever. Right, Neil?"

He had turned his head far away from her and back toward the house.

"Is the baby crying?" Elena asked. "I didn't hear her. Anyway, she's not crying now, Neil. Listen, let's play it the new way. It's more horribler, isn't it? Don't you like it? Stop now, Neil, don't laugh, it's dead serious, see? Come on, I mean it," and she touched the tips of her fingers to his knee. "See, Neil? Neil. What are you doing, Neil? Are you laughing? Are you? Neil? Laughing?"

A Lift

"Never pick up a hitchhiker," they had said over and over, she to her husband and he to her, and not just when they drove past one, either, but other times as well. Out of the comfort of their chairs on Sunday they would read aloud newspaper accounts of bad ends that had come to the foolish or unwary who did not follow such sensible advice. "Recent surveys taken on a major highway in Pennsylvania show 77 percent of all hitchhikers have previous criminal records," Mr. Horne read to her one morning, his voice excited with renewed alarm and certainty, and then, lowering his paper, he added seriously to her, as if she had never heard such a conclusion before, "Never pick up a hitchhiker."

"Never swim alone," they said, too, but with much less emotion, and when the children were young, "Don't fly on the same plane together," and as the years and decades passed, "Don't walk on ice." Sayings these were, and the others they used, that were proofs of Horne wisdom and Horne good sense. Sayings that were charms that had become worn with use from being passed back and forth to each other. And there was "Act your age," too, which only they understood correctly, and which meant how she dressed now when she went swimming or played golf, and which was in a gentle way a forgiveness for her aging.

They liked all their sayings, all their lighthearted or solemn talismans, all their signs of affection and invulnerability.

Yet he had died. Without any warning beforehand he had died. He had waked her in the night with a harsh gasp. Then he had gagged, and gagged horribly while she ran to the phone and to the bathroom and back to the bedroom again, banging and bruising her heavy body against the bedside table as she fumbled her way to him and knelt heavily by the bed, where he gagged and gagged against her while she pressed his head on her shoulder. He died before anybody came, and only she was left with him. She understood that he was dead. The doctor and the Norwegian neighbor from next door kept explaining this to her over and over, but it was not from bewilderment over what they were saying that she would not leave him until they twisted her fingers painfully loose from his hair and forced her up and away from him.

Her children, who were no longer children but married and long since parents, came to bury their father and to care for her. Yes, she told them both, she would visit them. Yes, she was fine. No, she would not move out of her apartment. Yes, they could talk to her banker. No, she would not move out, she was not going to do that. Yes, they could arrange the furniture. Yes, thank you for the television set. Yes, a single bed would be better. Yes, yes, yes.

She did go visit them, when they insisted. She drove the car to the home of one or the other child, no longer a child, and there unpacked her clothes for the few days of her visit. She got good at finding light switches in their unfamiliar houses. She made herself play with or talk to the grandchildren. She went to bed early to leave the living room free for the grown-ups. And what was she?

Then, when the committed days had passed, she returned home. There she would sit alone. Or she would go out in the afternoon to an art gallery with friends, and frequently on Wednesdays to lunch and the theater, with friends. She began to find she could not read, sitting alone. She began to find she was sitting waiting, and listening, and holding her breath. She got up and went by herself to the movies one night, quite late. She could not focus on the story, so much were all her senses sharpened to the dark silent presence of people around her. She clasped her handbag and stared unseeingly ahead and waited: everything was possible. When afterwards she had walked stiffly the long blocks to her apartment house, deliberately seeing nothing and no one but only the steps right before her,

A Lift

and had gone into her building and past the doorman and up in the elevator and was at last sitting in her own living room again, she took deep breaths through opened lips and reached with her hands for her face, felt the familiar/unfamiliar soft, pudgy skin and shook her head from side to side, unbelieving.

She went out again at night. She went to a movie first. When it was over she walked, even though it was raining, past her building and the open restaurant near it and around the corner to a street with two little coffeeshops on it, and a record store, and a pet shop that was closed, and a bar that was open, and a drugstore. She bought a sandwich but did not want it, and the thoughtful man wrapped it up for her in a doggie bag so she could take it home, and she came back to her apartment again just the same, absolutely safe.

It did not surprise her when she stopped for the hitchhiker. She was returning from a visit to her nearest daughter and driving the big car her husband had chosen for them. She saw the young man from some distance away and saw he had a sign with big black letters requesting the name of her city and stating he was from the college in the nearby town. He was tall, and as she came nearer she saw he had on one of those shirts that looked to her like condensed tennis nets. And his hair was long but not terribly long, and not curly. She was slowing the car as she came even with him, and he grinned and waved his hand at her. Never pick up a hitchhiker, she thought, and with a sudden burst of happiness said, "What idiocy."

She pulled off the highway and the wheels slipped and skidded unexpectedly. She clutched the wheel frantically and clung to it as the car slithered sideways and then jerked and stopped. She was not hurt, but went on clinging to the wheel, and the engine jumped again and died. In the rear-view mirror she saw the hitchhiker running toward her with his canvas bag in one hand and his sign, clutched under the other arm, banging and flapping against his leg. She reached down and started the engine and watched him running harder.

Then he was beside the car. He opened the door and bent down with his bag and his sign, and the heat from outside pushed through the coolness of the car's air-conditioning. She peered up at him. She saw that he was really very tall and young, and extremely clean and nice-looking, and his face was aglow with pleasure.

"Listen," he was saying to her. "I sure appreciate this. I really do."

She nodded and smiled back at him, feeling silly, feeling silly and awkward because she was bent down so that she could peer up at him out of the big, low car.

"Come in, get in," she said.

"Wow, air-conditioning. That's great," he said. He jammed his bag and sign on the floor between the front and middle seats. "This is great," he said. He beamed at her. He was delighted. And she saw that his eyes were really an intense deep gray, yet he seemed to her all one color, a light, light brown or gold color, like a piece of smooth sunbleached wood she had found on a beach.

"Listen, this is a terrific car," he said. He was sitting beside her now, and trying to arrange his big knees so he could shut the door. She drove with the seat pulled all the way forward since her husband's death, and there was not room for the length of his legs.

"There," he said. "I got myself folded in finally, didn't I? I'm pretty limber, I'll tell you," he turned around to look out the back window and then directed. "OK. You're clear. You can start now, but take it easy getting back onto the highway. You took a skid there, didn't you? You were going too fast when you pulled off. You shouldn't be doing more than four miles an hour getting on or off. OK, start slow."

She stared at him, then grasped the wheel so tightly the heavy rings on her fingers clicked against it. She drove the car carefully onto the highway. He was studying his watch. One of those intricate ones with a complexity of dials and hands that made her dizzy.

"Six and three-quarters minutes," he said. "That's about what I'd guessed, you know that? Six and three-quarters minutes." He was delighted. "How about that?" he asked her. "Listen, that breaks my record. Isn't that something? That's the fastest I've ever managed a ride. Once I hitched a ride in eleven minutes, but that was over a year ago now, and anyway, this was in only six and three-quarters minutes. Let's see, that's four and a quarter minutes better, to be exact." He beamed at her. "I always like to break my own records," he said. "Sometimes I really think I couldn't miss even if I tried. Which I don't." He laughed and ducked his head with charmed embarrassment. She took a quick, sideways glance at him while his head was down. She saw he had a strong round neck, and clean, shining hair lying loosely across the unwrinkled skin.

He took a deep breath of the cool air. "Air-conditioning. That's the ticket this time of year," he said. "Listen, I really appreciate your picking me up. The last time I hitched in the summer I rode in a green Chevy pickup. No air-conditioning there, you bet. No big problem, though, 'cause it wasn't terribly hot, and the man was nice. I really enjoyed riding with him. I had only four days that time, but I've got twelve days off now. I got ahead in my work so I can take off and not hurt my grades. I always plan to take my days off around holidays so I get extra time without bringing down my average. I'm an A student, you see," he said. He waited. "All A's," he added. "In everything. And I take some tough courses. Neat, hey?"

She smiled and nodded.

He shifted his legs in an effort to get more comfortable, and ended with one of them crossed high over the other and his long, thin foot dangling and jiggling cheerfully between them.

"I'm Bob Suddarth," he said. "Bob Ewart Suddarth." He beamed at the name. "That Ewart's something, isn't it? You're probably wondering about it."

"Not especially," she said.

"I don't mind," he went on. "People always ask me about it. You see, my dad, when he went to college, his best friend was Ewart. Yeah, L. D. Ewart. He's a contractor now. Well, my dad always said he'd name his first son after L. D. So when I came along, I was the first boy, you see, why he gave me the name Ewart, but as my middle name, see. That's how I came to have it." He beamed at her, charmed with these gifts he was giving her.

"My dad's like that," he said. "Does what he says he'll do, but makes it work. He's a great guy. Listen, excuse me, but you're sort of driving in both lanes, you know."

"Oh, I'm sorry," she said. She pulled the car over to the right.

This seemed somehow to bring her closer to him. She was aware of the length of him just there to her right, and of his foot jiggling close beside her.

"That's better," he said. "Yeah, my dad's really tops. You know he can do forty-two push-ups in a minute. Forty-two. I can do forty-five. Of course, I'll do better when I've built myself up more. I've started on a campaign to do that. I just made up my mind about it, just like that. You know, when I was in the eighth grade I made the same sort of decision about my chinning and—"

"I'm sorry about the driving," she interrupted.

"Don't feel bad," he said.

"I'm a poor driver. Some of my friends refuse to drive with me. I wouldn't be surprised if you felt the same way. I'd understand if you wanted to get out and ride with someone else."

"Oh, I don't feel that way a bit," he said. "I'll help you with your driving. It won't bother me at all, really. I won't mind. I've taught all kinds of people how to drive," and he beamed cheerfully at her.

She opened her mouth and then shut it again on the cool air-conditioned car air.

"You haven't told me your name yet," he said.

"Horne."

"Horne. Mrs. Horne. You haven't picked up many hitchhikers, have you? Yeah, I could tell, you know that? I really could, I could tell right off." And he ducked his head again, bemused by his own powers.

"Hitchhiking can be great for the experience," he went on. "Broadens you. Mostly two sorts of cars stop for hitchhikers. Nice cars, like yours, and old battered ones. Or trucks. Nothing in between. That's very interesting. Don't you think so?"

"Do you ever worry about who might be picking you up? Anyone at all might pick you up," she said.

"I never worry about that. I'm not the worrying type. Are you turning here?"

"Yes." She slowed the car.

A Lift

"And then going up 53?" he said. "Hey, I've never gone this way. What do you do, cross over at Kentland?"

"Yes. There's less traffic this way."

She made the turn and then picked up speed, and they were in pure farmland now. The highway ran straight for miles and corn and houses and telephone poles and corn and houses and telephone poles flipped by on either side.

"Sure," he said, "there would be less traffic this way. It's a wonder a lot more people don't do it."

"Then there wouldn't be less traffic," she said.

"You're right," he said, and laughed with pleasure and perfect amiability. She found herself smiling too. Why not? Oh, why not, he was so nice, so perfectly nice. There was a hint of some sort of odor in the car from him, not an unpleasant one, but there. Yet he was obviously so perfectly, perfectly nice.

"How old are you?" she asked. "Nineteen, perhaps? Sixteen and a half, maybe, and pretending to be older?"

"Hey, come on," he said. "I'm twenty. Well, just twenty. You got me there, I was twenty this July. July 4th. Isn't that something? I was born July 4th, just like this country."

"And you're going to college," she said.

"Yes, even in the summer. I'm pre-med, you see. I always wanted to be a doctor." He raised his arms overhead and folded them behind his neck and cradled his head. "Even when I was a little kid I wanted to be a doctor." He shook his head in fond, awed memory of himself. "I really did. I wanted a medical kit when I wasn't even in school yet, and I just wouldn't let anyone in the family have any peace until I got it. My mother says I gave every one of them examinations over and over, and the same with every visitor we had to the house. Can you imagine that? I always made them go into the bathroom, because it had all that white tile, you see, like a doctor's office, and then I'd give them my doctor's check-up routine. Isn't that something?"

"Didn't anyone ever turn you down?" she asked.

"No," he said, wobbling his head from its resting place on his arms. "No one ever did. The possibility never even occurred to me, I guess."

"Exactly, why would it," she said. *"Mens vacua in corpore sano,* right?"

"What?"

"Nothing, you wouldn't understand." But he might have, she thought; good heavens, he might have.

He turned his face to the window and looked out at the fields of corn. "Will you look at that corn," he said. "It must be ten feet high already. Richest land in the U.S. My dad's in farm implements. He sells the best farm equipment made, and he says this is the best farmland there is. He's said that ever since I can remember."

"How nice for you," she said. She must stop this.

"My uncle," he went on, "he's my mother's brother, not my dad's, he's in farm machine repairs. He's in farm building construction, too, and in farm supplies. With all that in the family, you'd think I'd go into farm supplies and equipment, wouldn't you? But no, I was determined to be a doctor. Never budged about it a bit. Not for a minute. That's interesting, isn't it?"

"Fascinating," she said.

He stopped talking this time. She felt a stab of satisfaction. She should not, she told herself, but she did.

"The corn's pretty when it tassels, isn't it?" he commented after a minute, looking through the glass of the window. "I don't know anything that's prettier. Tassels look just like silk, don't they?"

She pressed her lips shut and kept silent.

"Listen," he said, "I just noticed. Your air-conditioner drips. Probably not insulated right. When we stop, I'll look at it."

"I never let anyone fool around with my car," she said.

"I don't blame you. But I've worked in my uncle's shop, you see, and I know what I'm doing. In fact, I can fix almost anything once I set my mind to it. I have a sort of sixth sense about what's wrong with a machine. If I can do that in medicine, have that sort of sixth sense but with people, not machines, and then have all the science stuff too, why I'll clean up. And be a good doctor. Then, when I've

A Lift

made my pile, I'm going to travel. This is fine country around here, but I've been born and raised in it, so I want to travel everywhere else. It's natural to want to do that, and I'm going to. In fact, I'm going to do a million things."

"You don't exactly suffer from lack of confidence, do you?"

"Why should I?" he said. He laughed and ducked his head. "No, why should I? You know what they say, confidence makes the man."

"If you're simpleminded enough to believe it."

"Listen, why jump on me?" he said. "You've done it a couple of times already, you know that? I haven't done anything to you. I mean, why pick on me, you don't even know me!"

She could not answer him. He was right. Why didn't she just quit it? Or why didn't she stop, instead? She could stop the car, and tell him she could not take him any farther and ask him to get out.

"Hey," he said, delight lifting his voice. "There's a train coming ahead. We'll have to wait for it and it's going to be a long one, too. I can tell. Look, there goes the old signal." He was alert and eager, his face shining, glowing with interest, and absolutely smooth. "Listen to it coming. Look at those cars. They've got some of the new ones, see, right there, those long ones. They're cushioned. There, that's another one, did you see it? It's a cushioned car. What a great idea. I wonder who thought of it? Bet he made a pile off of it. You know, I once counted eighty-seven cars on one of these freight trains. Can you imagine that? Eighty-seven. This one's going to be close to that, I bet. Thirteen already and I can't see the end of it at all. The corn's in the way, though. It's going pretty slow, too. Must be a gradient here. Yeah, I guess that's it. Well, I might as well not waste my time counting cars but get busy and look at this air-conditioner of yours."

"Don't," she said. "I don't want you to," but he was bending down and under the slender rectangle of the air-conditioner. He was curling and winding under and around it, and his head was almost out of sight.

"You should have got the built-in kind, you know?" he said from underneath. "They work better. Do you know that? You should tell that to your husband. You know?" He was speaking loudly since she had not answered.

"We never used the car in the summer," she said. "We always went away in the summer. Please, please don't fool with it. Please. I don't want you to."

"I won't hurt a thing, really I won't. Listen, this air-conditioner hasn't been put in right, either. I bet your husband doesn't know much about cars, now does he? Huh? Does he?"

"No," she said. She leaned her head heavily against the window of her car. "No, he doesn't."

"What does he do? Mrs. Horne? What's he do?" He was almost shouting, as if she had not answered because she could not hear him.

"He's in fertilizer," she said, and grinned. And then said again, speaking as loudly as he, almost shouting, "He's in fertilizer."

"He is?" His head emerged. "Really? Listen, an outlet, or a territory?" He was all interest, all bright and smooth and golden interest.

"A territory," she said, and her mouth stretched helplessly and painfully wider and wider. "He's in a territory," she told him.

He inched his head even farther out to get an unbroken view of her. "Why, I'll bet my dad knows him," he said. "My dad knows everyone. Horne. Horne. Sure, I'll bet my dad knows him."

He rested his cheek reflectively against the rectangular box of the air-conditioner. He was bent and curled like a sapling, like a vine, around it. How clear his face was. How beautiful the skin beside the black of the metal. How soft and hard both his flesh was. And his eyelids fit so smoothly at the corners.

"Yes, I bet my dad knows him," he said. Then he moved and disappeared again beneath the metal box and after a minute he called out, "It *is* the insulation. Just like I said it was. Suddarth's right again. You know, I can't lose for winning. I should be in this business. It needs rewrapping, that's all. I'll do it for you next filling station."

He emerged and straightened up in the seat. "Still choo-choo train cars, I see," he said. "Listen, you getting tired? Just relax. It won't take much longer, then we can go on. Tell me, what's your husband's first name? So I can ask my dad if he knows him."

"Jerome."

"Jerome? Oh, you mean Jerry?"

"No, Jerome. Jerome Horne. You know," she said, grinning again, wider and wider, "you know, like in blow your own horn."

"Hey, that's funny, Mrs. Horne," he said. "That's really good, you know, it's funny. Listen, listen, you don't look good. Want me to drive?"

"No," she said.

"I think I better drive. You don't look good at all. You know what I mean? I mean you don't look like you feel at all well."

"No," she said. "I feel fine. I don't want you to drive."

"Look, it's no trouble. You just move over real easy. I'll walk around to your side of the car and get in, then I'll drive us."

"No," she said.

"Then I'll turn the car around right here," he had his hand on the handle, he was opening the door, "and I can do that easy. It's no problem for me to make a turn like that, don't worry about that. I'll turn around and drive back to the first filling station. And I'll call your husband for you. You really don't look good, and I'll explain that to him and tell him what happened and why I drove and everything like that."

"You can't, you fool," she said. "He's dead."

"He's dead? Dead?" He closed the car door, shutting them both in. "Then he . . . listen, that's a terrible thing to do, to say that he was in fertilizer like that. That's a terrible thing. You shouldn't say that sort of thing about your own husband, especially if he's dead. I mean, it isn't nice. How do you think he'd feel?"

"He doesn't feel," she said.

"Listen, Mrs. Horne, stop grinning like that. It isn't funny. You shouldn't be grinning about it. It's a sad thing if he doesn't feel."

"You fool. You fool, look at you sitting there going on and on babbling about your precious self and watching yourself when you can in the mirror, oh yes, I saw you doing that. I know you, admiring the way you look and the light on your skin, I know. Go on doing it, go on babbling about yourself and your charms and praising yourself and being in love with yourself, it doesn't matter because it's waiting for you, too. And it's eating on you, too, already. All the time, all the time, since you were born it's waiting for you, a crocodile lying waiting for you. And it takes a bite here and a bite there, yes it does, yes it does and it waits, and it'll turn you into someone just like me. Oh yes it will, you'll see, you'll get soft and old and pudgy the way I am, and you'll be foolish and silly and fatuous, too, just the way I am, with the crocodile waiting for more and more of you until you rot away, until you're just like me."

His face was horrified. All the blandness, all the niceness gone out of it. And she was pleased, oh she was pleased. She could measure by the shock in his eyes how pleased she was and her fingers curled and tightened so harshly on the steering wheel that the heavy rings pressed achingly into the flesh of her fingers.

"Get out," she said.

"I can't do that," he said. "You just relax now. I'm going to help you, Mrs. Horne."

"Get out," she yelled at him. "Get out of my car, you fool, just get out."

"No, I can't do that. It wouldn't be right with you like this. I have to help you, and that's what I'm going to do."

"You take your stinking little prick and get out of my car."

He gaped at her. "You're crazy," he said. "You're plain crazy."

"Take it and get out," she said. "You stink. And it stinks, too."

"I'll be glad to," he said. "Listen, it'll be a pleasure to get away from you."

He opened the door wide and the hot air, gathered and held tight by the tall corn, rushed inside the car and around them. The train had gone on by them without their noticing, and there was quiet in the hot air outside.

"I'll get another ride," he said. He was tugging his canvas bag to get it out. "I never have any trouble getting rides. I can always get them." He tugged again on his bag but it was jammed. In his efforts to find room for his legs he must have pushed his side of the front seat back and jammed the bag. He jerked and pulled at it, but he could not get it free.

"Use the latch to move the seat," she told him in a muttered aside, as if she were not really speaking to him.

A Lift

"I can't find the latch," he said back to her in the same way. "I can't find it anywhere."

"It's toward the back. There, it's on your side but toward the back. That's it."

He had found it, and he moved the seat forward enough to pull his bag loose. "There," he said as he got it out. And then in released fury he said, speaking loudly again, "OK, there. Only I'll be damn careful who I ride with next time, I'll tell you."

She put her hand on the shift to start the car, but he held on to the door of the car.

"Wait a minute," he said. "I want my sign." He reached in for it carefully, watching to make sure she did not start the car on him. "There," he said, when he had it. "I've got it." His face was shining now, gleaming, and his eyes were the same intense clear gray they had been when she first saw him.

"Listen, you want to know something?" he said, holding the door firmly open. "You can go on alone even if you are sick and I don't care. You know why? Because you're a terrible woman."

No, no, she shook her head. No.

"Oh yes, you are. A terrible, terrible old woman. I'm sorry to say that, but you are."

She shook her head. Shook her head as he slammed the door hard into the car. It wasn't true. She started the car moving forward, driving away from him, going up and over the soft bumps of the railroad tracks and driving on between the cornfields and the farms and the telephone poles. It wasn't true. She was not terrible. That was the terrible thing, that she was not terrible. "God forgive me, God forgive me," she whispered, shaking her head, and the windshield dissolved and wavered and wept before her eyes as she shook her head and shook her head. There was no forgiveness, she knew; there was only the crocodile.

Luz

I ran errands in my neighborhood. From the time I was two days past four years old and could decode the red and green of streetlights at the corner I maneuvered on my own through the concrete world of blocks that stretched ahead of me in all directions, seemingly without end. With age and experience I learned the limits of my larger territory: blacks ten blocks to the west; the river's edge bounding the far east; rich white street-empty apartments to the north; and pure commerce to the south. By the time I knew the boundaries, I had discovered that a boy alone is welcome to his neighbors. They would send me on errands, and they would pay me. I found there was good money in it.

An old man in our building, a huge man, over six feet, maybe six feet six, sent me to get his lady friend. Luz was her name. He would send me for her in the early evening or late afternoon, when his wife was out. He had a badly crippled leg clamped in a full metal brace and he could not get around easily even in his own rooms. There was no phone in his apartment and I could see he was not able to get out by himself to telephone Luz, but he never wanted me to, either. He wanted messages sent. I don't know why. Perhaps her messy room, the edges of which I came to know, also had no phone and no one in her building would take calls for her. And maybe the beauty parlor where I went for her in the afternoons did not want her getting personal calls when she should be working. Whatever, my old crippled man would call to me from his landing as I passed and give me three or four coins and tell me to go to her. He always sent the same message.

"Tell her the freezer's melted," he would say.

Luz would laugh no matter how many times she had heard it. She was always in a good humor, but when she laughed she would show her sharp, snapping teeth. She, too, would give me a coin or two, and in the winter, for good measure, she would pull my cap down over my ears and massage with her strong skilled beauty operator's fingers the deliciously relaxing back of my neck.

Luz was half Mexican and had the thick black molasses-like hair she could layer in whorls, or drape flat across her head, or pile high as a sand castle with a rose stabbed in it.

"I know what her name means in our language," I told the old man one evening when he wanted me to go for her. "It means light."

But I never once asked him to pay me for not telling his wife, though when I took messages to Luz I did look everywhere, in the grocery store, at the bus stops, for a glimpse of what I knew to be his wife's old blue dress or that brown coat she wore even past when it was needed. I never saw her then.

I tracked Luz often after I took her messages and she did go on those days to my old man in my own building. And times when I was doing nothing better I ran ahead of her and was on my own landing two floors above and watching when she came. Old crip would be there waiting for her with the door wide open and himself doused in lotion to cover his old sick man smell. I did not know what she saw in my old ailing man with his brace, but I knew, even before I was ten, that if he paid her it was not the same as his paying me, for she did not go to him only for money.

She went for laughter, I decided. For I could hear them chuckling and giggling and hooting when the door shut opaque and solid behind them. She went for laughter. When I saw her on the sidewalk afterward, for sometimes I would hang around and wait until she came out, her caramel skin would be blushed with humor and her lips relaxed from smiling and her eyes coal-black and popping like the round, polished, not-yet-burning coals in the Japanese restaurant on the corner.

The summer I turned ten I learned to know Luz better, for I was hired, illegally at my age, by her beauty parlor's owner to sweep the floor of the limp, cut curls and polish shelves of vivid colored bottles and, as ever, to run errands—this time to get coffee and sandwiches. I kept my old errand business on the side to have that money too. I did very well, for the neighborhood, so low in telephones, was infested with messages. Some were legal, some not, and I trotted through the litter and the people of the summer streets carrying names or numbers that for the sender had the aura of riches, carrying payments of bills and promises of money, and carrying sandwiches, cokes, and coffee for the customers and staff in the beauty parlor.

The regular customers I soon learned and what they usually ordered, and I learned the customers who were steadies for Luz. One of them I corrected.

"Her name's not said that way," I insisted. "It's like 'loose' in 'loose change.' 'Luz.'"

Because I no longer came home after school, my old crippled buddy could not call out to me when I passed his landing. So from the beauty parlor Luz would send me to my building. There I was to stay on the landing below the old boy's door and whistle a tune loudly enough for him to hear. If his wife was out, he would open the door and give me the message about his freezer.

Luz amused herself by changing the tune. Sometimes she had me whistle the "Star-Spangled Banner," sometimes a Christmas carol, sometimes a Mexican bullfight song she would try, between combing out customers, to teach me by pretending she was playing the harsh Mexican trumpet.

She laughed at each different tune she suggested, as if she were pulling a joke that was even better than changing the way she fixed her black, glossy, treacle-like hair. Luz was always good-natured. But details and routines of the beauty parlor business would bore her and her eyes would rise to the street, to life going by her out there. Then she would send me to my building to whistle her latest tune, and perhaps, perhaps the old man would open his door and give me the right report on his freezer's state of being, and also give me one or two coins to put deep down in my pocket.

I would run back to Luz in the beauty parlor, and if the message was right, she would greet it with delight in shining, effervescent eyes. She would finish with her customer, and as soon as she could rearrange her appointments clip-clop on her bright polished heels down the dirty street to our building. I liked to watch her walking. She had

Luz

slim, shapely legs despite her solid body. Unlike the other operators, she had no varicose veins and she never wore pants. I do not know if she followed a Latin custom or vanity, but she wore only skirts and black or white blouses, to exaggerate, I believed, her black, snapping eyes. When I could think of a reason to get away from the beauty parlor, I would follow her all the way to our building.

Our entrance was more elaborate than any other in the block. There were figures of animals and decorative whorls that were like Luz's hair except they were in worn white concrete. The figures entertained Luz, and invariably on her way in she ran a finger over one bird's nose and poked its eye. She had a practical cruelty about animals. I never saw her pet a dog and often heard her rage against people feeding pigeons, and the only attention I ever saw her give any beast was to poke the concrete eye of the bird in our entrance and mutter a Spanish word at it and laugh.

Yet she was kind to me. When she sent me with a message she always paid me, and often she gave me parts of her lunch. I took these and ate them. Then I did not have to spend any money buying my lunch.

It was inevitable that the day came when the old man was ill, but still it was a shock to me. I had not thought about anything inevitable. I whistled and whistled Luz's Spanish dancer's tune (part of her people's real national anthem, she told me) on the landing, but the old boy's door never opened until, to my surprise, a white-haired old lady came out. She was old crip's wife, Mrs. Schnelling. I recognized her face though mostly I had seen only her back, shoving in our building door when her arms were loaded with flat boxes of envelopes she and the old boy stuffed to make a living.

She squiggled a finger and uncomfortably I moved closer to her. She told me in a whisper that old braced-leg was bad sick. And she was scared. I was to hurry up medicine from the drugstore, for he had told her, she said to me, when he heard all that racket I was making, that I often helped with his medicine. So I was to do just what I always did, he had told her to say.

Clearly she thought I usually acted out of brotherly love and the relationship was based on my generosity, fondness, pure goodwill, and kindness. For even though I waited, she made no move to give me money.

A little sour, for I did not see how I was going to be paid by her, I forgot the part about the medicine. I had never in my life brought him medicine. Instead I set out to do what I knew the old boy meant for me to do. I ran down the stairs and out of our entrance, and, as I always did, skipped the last worn stone steps not to add my weight to what had been done already. I ran straight to the beauty parlor. I got Luz aside and told her the news.

To my ten-year-old astonishment, tears as easily as laughter broke from her eyes and spattered down her face. I was overwhelmed. I had been going to explain to her, I had already decided on it, that no one had paid me yet because I knew Luz would. But it did not seem right to ask her while she went on weeping right there in the beauty parlor for anyone to see, weeping for the cripple-legged old man who was her companion in locked-in laughter.

What had they done, I wondered as she cried, that had made her love this laughing so much? That old man's apartment must have been just like my family's two floors above it. There was nothing that great about ours, with its tight square rooms that looked out across a clogged air space at a brick building, just as the old man's must.

Luz wiped her face, smearing her eye stuff and tossing the blackened towel in the laundry bin. She begged another operator to fit in two customers, and then, on her trim legs, Luz trotted out onto the street and toward our building.

"I forgot to tell the delicatessen no tomatoes," I shouted at the owner working in the rear. He never knew what I was talking about, only that I kept his customers filled with food and drinks and the floor swept clean. He nodded and I followed to catch up with Luz. It was easy for me to do as my sight was not masked in tears, but every half-block she had to stop and wipe hers away while people walking on the street bumped into her. She turned into the entrance of our building, this time without pecking the bird's worn nose.

Like all the buildings on the block, the staircase looped back and forth against one wall and the hallways and apartments clung to the opposite side. The stairs were narrow with steep steps, but Luz ran up as if her high heels were runner's sneakers.

I was in a quandary. I dared not follow so close I got myself caught, yet I had to be there when that door opened. I was weasel-thin that summer. By squeezing my body into the narrow space around which the stairway made its turn at every landing I believed I could sneak my head level with the Schnellings' floor without being noticed. I balanced myself on the handrail that sloped below their landing and slid my fingers around the spokes sunk in the floor above. I gently lifted my head up in the slot between the banisters. There before me, visible through the spokes, were Luz's red and highly polished heels.

Now at the door, Luz was hesitating for the first time, not to wipe her tears but unsure of what to do. She may never have come here before when the door was shut. All the times I had watched, old crippled-leg had been standing there, braced and lotioned, announcing their time had come and that he had heard her feather step floating its way to him. He would be grinning away as he said it, his face pale as uncooked bacon. Life inside had bleached him, yet he was always smiling for her. What they had to laugh at I could never think.

Luz shifted back and forth on her high heels. I raised my head higher, level with her ankles, so I could really see.

With the ringing sure sound she made clapping the cut ends of hair out of a brush rapped against the washbasin, Luz knocked on the door in a series of taps. I was startled enough to slip down, then raised myself up to see.

The door opened the chained few inches, and old Mrs. Schnelling looked out. Even from my angle, peering, I could see how frightened she looked.

"You're not the doctor from the welfare clinic," Mrs. Schnelling said first thing. "I know them. Why hasn't one come? I called twice my husband's so bad. I went upstairs two times to call."

Upstairs? From *my* apartment? My home? Home, I'd learned when I was four years old, is where you run to when you crap in your pants. But my mother was usually out, working, or if at home was cleaning house, and she was never friendly with the neighbors. Mrs. Schnelling must have gone to another floor, or another apartment. Not my home.

"I am the social worker," I heard Luz lie. And in her white beauty parlor operator's coat it seemed possible. To Mrs. Schnelling anything may have seemed possible in our neighborhood. She shut the door, took off the chain, and opened the door wide.

"I didn't send for a social worker," she said.

"I have come because there is needing," Luz said. Her English was heavily accented. "All these blocks is my areas," she said, with the sublime air of confidence with which she would shear a thick length of hair with one twist of her wrist and a prolonged steady swishing of her cutting scissors. "All these blocks I am inspector," she finished. Very positive.

I jiggled on the banister. Was she going to bluff and bully her way inside into the old man's sickroom? And if she did, if they went inside, how was I going to see? I could never get around to the fire escape in time, and anyway I already knew it did not work.

From the inside of the apartment came the old boy's voice.

"Is that the doctor?" he called. He sounded terrible.

"No," Luz said instantly, lifting her voice and tossing it like a javelin into their home. "Just your own neighborhood's excellent and esteemed social worker who hearing you had a not-well feeling made the appearance. Yes?"

There was a period of silence which could have been filled by either woman but was not. Then, unexpectedly to them both, the old boy, all six foot plus and brace, appeared beside his wife. He was wearing a bright blue terry-cloth robe wrapped loosely around his body, and his gray chest was a strangely virgin field peeping out behind it. From my weasel's perch I could see he was red-eyed and unsteady, and that his face was blurred by his unshaven beard. That's a man only a wife has to love, I thought, and I turned and gazed up to see what my beauty parlor operator was going to do.

Luz had let her head tip to the side, as if overcome by the weight of her magnificent dark hair piled in a double soft-ice-cream-cone spiral.

"I could bring you the juices," she said to him.

"I asked the boy to do that," Mrs. Schnelling said. It was a lie. She had not. "How did you get your brace on by yourself," she said, scolding, to terry-cloth robe. "You shouldn't be out of your bed."

The old boy was clinging hard to the door frame beside her. If they took a notion and closed that door, I thought, they were going to crush his fingertips.

"I give the help for the medicines. Or for the othercoming procedures," Luz said. Those last long words, I knew, were proud new acquisitions.

"I suppose you got that job because you speak Mexican," Mrs. Schnelling said.

For it was amazing how official that white jacket made Luz seem. But that was not helping old crip. He was trembling in the doorway and grasping the frame with his finger edges.

"When I need you," he said, and his voice sounded like a record being scratched, "I'll send the boy with a message. I'll be able to do that soon. Soon."

His unshaven, uncombed head vibrated not unlike the hand massager in the beauty parlor, but in his case from some inner lack of power.

"I can do nothings now?" Luz asked him.

"I suppose your Mexican is better than your English," Mrs. Schnelling said.

Old crip did not answer. He was concentrating on holding onto that door frame. Luz, with an elegant shrug, was about to turn, and I was lowering my head so I could drop to the landing below, when the old boy gave a juicy grunt and lurched forward. He would have fallen but Luz, with a beauty parlor operator's speed (two seconds and a rinse is a ruin, she had taught me), was holding him up.

Mrs. Schnelling came under his arm and tried to lever him back up to the doorway while closing his flapping robe around him, but the brace and its clumsiness and the old boy's size made it impossible. He had nothing above him now that he could reach for, if he had been able, to help raise himself upright. Luz's elegant legs were beginning to go under with his weight, and I let myself slide down to the floor beneath and raced back up the stairs. I burst in between the two women and like a tugboat began pushing our giant upright, and I chattered all the time about how I had just happened to get home, which was natural enough as I did live right there, upstairs, I said, so near.

"Thank you, thank you," Mrs. Schnelling said, but Luz cast me one long look, black and unwinding as a screwdriver's action. She knew how come I was there.

Having stopped old crip from falling, the problem with his brace was turning him around. He was helpless, sweating and groaning. Mrs. Schnelling kept saying she and I could manage, she and I could do it alone. But old crip had a death grip on Luz's neck, so the four of us jammed and juggled and then popped through the doorway into the apartment and we lowered, slowly, the old boy's long body to the floor.

Mrs. Schnelling began to tug at his robe to get it over the gray matted hair on his chest.

"He should not have come to the door," Mrs. Schnelling said. She tried to free the robe, which was crumpled under him. "He should have stayed in bed. Give some help, now you are here," she said to Luz.

But Luz's head was clutched to the old man's half-bared shoulder, and he held on to her so tightly she could do nothing.

"Is that what my taxes do?" Mrs. Schnelling asked. "Can't you help? It's a disgrace," she said, all the while pulling at her husband's robe to cover him with it.

"Here, Luz," I said, "I'll help you." I tried to lift the old boy's arm, but he whimpered aloud and clung to her.

"No, no," Luz said to me, "let's him go," and then, "now watch. I took the yoga. Watch what I doing."

She was so pleased I thought she meant to untangle his octopus grasp but instead she swung her bottom around sideways and flexed her neck and arm and shoulder so she was half sitting, half bending; she was like a lily, with her head and its dome of black hair with the bright, plastic rose still pressed tight on his shoulder. She had a satisfied smile on her face after her exertions.

Mrs. Schnelling was busy trying to slide the blue terry-cloth robe between the old boy's shoulder and Luz's face. Luz, as willingly as she followed her customers' suggestions on their hair styles, tried to raise her head enough to provide the needed space.

"He has much force," Luz said in a conversational way. But Mrs. Schnelling was occupied elsewhere.

The old boy was whispering to her. I was close enough so I could hear him. He wanted a handkerchief, he whispered. He wanted her to help him straighten the teeth in his head and to wipe his mouth clean. Old Mrs. Schnelling got up and came back with a cloth and wiped his lips for him with it. Then she let him use her fingers to shove his upper plate in and press it up and tight into place while he held fast to Luz with his more deft right hand.

"You," Mrs. Schnelling said to Luz, "you do nothing at all. You are a disgrace."

The old boy had his face ready and he turned it to Luz, and when he did the corners of his mouth climbed up like roses on the trellis of the wrinkles in his face.

I was ten, then, and I knew everything there was to know about sex. But when I saw the corners of his mouth climb up I wished I had four eyes and two heads to watch them both constantly so every single thing that was going on between them I could see.

Old crip began gasping and gurgling, making sounds like a fluttering refrigerator. And his chest started going hugely up and down, and up up up, reaching for something.

"Oh why don't they come?" Mrs. Schnelling cried. "I told them twice they need to come instantly." And she stood there alone beside him, watching his chest.

"Ah ah ah," the old boy was gasping to Luz, "tell . . . tell . . ." he said, and with her face held close to his, Luz began to tell.

"Oh, they are so funny, the women," Luz said. "The foolish vain women," and the old boy's breathing eased in its gasping. "Never are there so much vanities," Luz said, forgetting she was supposed to be a social worker and not a beauty parlor operator in that white coat.

I watched and watched old Mrs. Schnelling to see what she would do when she noticed, but she was lost in gauging the breathing in her husband's body.

"Always trying to win the mens," Luz was saying. "They do everything to win the mens." How he smiled, how pleased he was when she said that. "They make the hair orange or purple if the hair comes by itself white. They do whatsoever to please the mens. And the creams, oh for the face they use so much bottles of creams you can't believe."

Luz halted in telling because the old boy's chest had begun mounting and falling and the struggling refrigerator sound had started from him again. Luz looked around for Mrs. Schnelling, but Mrs. Schnelling had rushed into the other room. The old boy gave Luz a pull, a nudge—meaning, get on with the story.

"Yes, yes," Luz said, "there is no ending the vanities. There is the woman today who coats with powder ten times thick, like this," and Luz patted her cheek and then the cheek nearest to old crip, in the way a woman might in making herself up before a mirror, and old wrinkle-jaws pulled his lips wide in his amusement. "Oh to get the mens they use much vanities," Luz said.

He was enthralled, enthralled, and yet even so he was beginning to shiver all over his long body and his brace made a slender vibrating noise against the floor and his chest reached up and up a mountain.

Mrs. Schnelling came hurrying back into the room with an old gray blanket she was shaking clear of moth crystals, and she tumbled it across him and began to wrap it around his quivering body, bundling him up tight as a mummy.

Even I, who had never seen anything bad sick but animals, knew the old boy must be dying, and that nothing was going to change that, not even the blanket with glittering bits of moth crystals.

"Why don't the doctors come," Mrs. Schnelling pleaded as she wrapped his legs, folding the blanket double over them. "God, let a doctor come," she said. She knelt to bundle the upper part of the man's body and, kneeling there, covering him, said, "Let the real help I called for come."

"Mrs.," Luz said to her, "please. Don't wrap him two times up. It has no need. He is not cold that way."

The old boy's arm no longer clasped Luz's neck tight, and though he still held to her, she could straighten herself.

"Sit instead, Mrs.," Luz said to Mrs. Schnelling. "Sit there beside," meaning beside old crip. "Take a cushion to yourself to sit comfortable so you can give comfort for him."

The old boy was giving Luz tugs with his arm, which was limper now, which held her even more loosely. But he wanted her to get on with her story.

Luz

"So like always my Tuesday-morning-at-ten come," Luz began again. "And this time she want a teenager's hair style, to make her beautiful. Can you believe? Out of our twenties is this style, out of Egypt before, with the hair curled down on the cheeks in baby circles so," and Luz traced with her expert fingers on his wrinkles where the curls were meant to go, and the old boy was enchanted, I could see it, yet even so his chest pumped and climbed up its mountain and he gurgled in air.

Mrs. Schnelling had got herself down on a cushion by old crip's other side, but his gasping got harsher as his chest rose, and she plugged her hands against her mouth.

"No, Mrs., please. No." Luz said to her, in the exact tone she used to the littler girls when they cried for the locks that they could see in the mirror they were going to lose. "No, Mrs. Take his hand in yours two, please, and rub in the way you are both using all the years, and with force, so he will know is you doing it."

"Yes," Mrs. Schnelling said, "yes," and she unwound old crip's hand from its mummy wrappings.

She shoved back his terry-cloth robe and laid his bared and long old arm across her lap and stroked the length of it. The old boy's head trembled toward her and he turned up his hand at the hinge of his wrist and took the edge of her sleeve in his cumbersome fingers. How with those fingers he had folded papers and stuffed envelopes, unless she had done it all, I don't know. But he began to roll and massage the edge of her sleeve between his fingers and the palm of his hand.

His head wobbled back toward Luz and she took up her story.

"I tell you also about that Keyes woman. Oh, she is foolish. So foolish you can't believe." The old man's face was setting itself to smile. "For much months this foolish woman she is keeping all her curls, no matters the colors. She is keeping them, she say, for the fall of hair she will make, a twist you see, to braid and put in a net for wearing. But the colors I say to her, you dye you hair all differing colors."

The old man's chest was lumbering on its climb with the air gurgling harshly in and Luz began to hurry her story.

"So you know what this foolish woman say to me? You can't believe," Luz said, and she began to sway as she told her story, rocking his body along with her. Old Mrs. Schnelling smoothed her husband's arm and with her head bent close to his hand watched his fingers slowly working the material of her sleeve. "This woman say," Luz went on, "she will dye all the curls one color. Black, the exact color mine comes. She will braid them to wear exact the way I display mine. Can you believe?"

Old crip seemed to want to laugh at it, too. He seemed starting to laugh, but the laugh was a hawk in his throat, and Luz rocked on, taking him with her and rushing her story to its end, saying, "To wear it like I do? Why? And she say, oh, can you believe? she say then she will look just like me," and the old boy's arm was sliding down her back, his arm let her free, but she went on rocking his body, telling, "Such a foolishness. I know she is exact sixty years old, this vain woman, and I say why does she want it her hair like mine? And she say she want because, she tell me, I am beautiful. Can you believe? Beautiful."

Luz began to giggle at her own story, to rock his long still body and giggle, but her eyes were weeping, were glossy and glimmering and weeping. And I thought, if that's how her tears make her eyes look while laughing, if that's what her tears can do then, she should patent them now, I thought. She could make her fortune.

The Calling

He believed in God in Vermont. The trees made the difference. The trees, and the people. The people did not steal. And they wanted a minister. On his second day he was called to Alma Ferguson's bedside to pray for her recovery, and when he did two other members of the family followed him into the bedroom and bowed their heads along with him as he read the service beside her ancient, pointed knees. When it was finished, the blessing given, and he was standing on the street by his car with his prayer book in his hand and his white collar visible as the hand of God around his throat, passersby in cars looked out their windows at him with approval. So stunned was he by this after the city, so astonished, that he dallied by the car, fumbling with the handle, to savor the experience.

In New York, his vestments had been stolen. And later, his car. He had been second-in-charge of a large youth center, but it was not youths who came, it was grown men. Young enough, but men all the same—dropouts, criminals, gang members who were smart-aleck and cynical and into drugs. The scum of the streets he had left behind when he crawled up by reading and hard work, and he better than anyone knew that youths like the one he had been were locked in small corners of their homes, trying to study. None of the ones who came to the center wanted what he could give them. He tried telling himself they were using him as God's instrument unknowingly and that should be enough, but it was not.

"I can love a thief as well as the next man can," he told his bishop. "So long as he steals because he's poor and wants to get ahead, or even because he wants some crummy thing he can't afford to buy. But these bums don't steal for reasons like that. They steal to take away. Not to have, but to keep someone else from having. To wreck. I grew up among them, and I know them. Listen, my car was smashed into a thousand pieces by them. They even took the bolts off and stripped them. It must have taken hours. If they put that much work into studying they could all go to Harvard."

"It's because you have these links with them that we need you here," the Bishop said. The Bishop was young and good-looking, relaxed and sure of his touch.

"I don't think we're doing a single thing right," he replied to the Bishop. "We're missing the good ones, the ones we can help. Hell, they're so scared of the crooks we've got in our center they'd never come near it. The ones we've got what they need is the . . . hell beaten out of them. Listen, our ice-hockey team took their own gear and sold it. You need someone else for my place, someone who can believe in these creeps. Maybe my kind of faith is worse than none."

"Try. Try again. You're too hard on yourself," the Bishop said smoothly, "far too hard." But the next year, after the youth center was burned to the ground and only four twisted girders stood like thick, dazed cobras, the Bishop decided to send him to Vermont.

"It's little pay for you," the Bishop told him. "And to be perfectly honest, not much future. But it will be your own church, and it is only one, not a jointure of two small churches, or even three. You'll like the maple syrup. It's dirt-cheap there. You might send me a can. One of those half-gallon ones. Around Christmastime, say."

Alma Ferguson died. When he mounted the pulpit to preach her funeral service it was to the first full church he had ever seen before him. He had to force himself not to gape, so astonishing was the crowd. It contained all sizes and ages, and included even serious and wealthy men sitting ready to listen to him. Later, at the cemetery, there were so many followers that the responses to his calls to prayer came in solid walls of sound around him in the cold air. It was fall,

The Calling

and early morning, and so clear the mountains jumped close when he glanced up at them and the outlines of trees looked like sharp, jagged cuts in the glass-blue sky. He bent far forward over the grave, crumbling the bits of rocky soil onto the coffin, and shut his eyes tight and prayed for the resurrection of the dead.

"I've found home," he said to his landlady. She always looked slightly to the left of him in conversation. She brought him bread and glazed doughnuts she made, and he paid her carefully each time, knowing it was Yankee and correct to do so, but sure it had more meaning than mere money. She was not even in his church. "I've never seen such beautiful country," he said, speaking to her right cheek. "It's like coming home."

"Home's where the heart is," she said.

He wanted nothing. His vestry could not believe it. He was young (thirty-four, he had written on the form; six feet, four inches; weight left blank; this his first church; born in N.Y.C.). He asked for no new buildings. Not even plans to begin one. No additional or professional Sunday-school teachers, no repairs to the broken P.A. system, not even new hymnals to place in his napkin-peaked white church. He was ecstatic with their services. He did not want to introduce sex education into the kindergarten or "God-is-dead" books in the adult discussion groups, nor lecture on V.D. and drugs to the teenagers. He wasn't even interested in having Saturday night movies to raise money and bring them in touch with the realities of the modern world.

"Jesus, if you'll excuse the expression, what's he going to do with his time?" That was Blakeless. He usually spoke first at informal vestry meetings. He was the only farrier ever to be on the vestry. He had made a fortune.

"Worried you won't get your money's worth again?" Simmons asked. Simmons was the druggist. He owned and ran the drugstore. He knew every man's illness. He was soft and white, and wore thick, rimless glasses as round and shiny as the bottoms of apothecary bottles.

"We could have shared him with West Fairfield and split the salary," someone said.

"We've always had our own minister," said another. There were ten of them gathered this night.

"With the money we could have made a down payment on an organ. We're probably the only Episcopal church there is without an organ."

"I didn't know you were so musical."

"Shut up, Simmons."

"He's the tallest minister we've ever had. I thought cities bred them small."

"I wonder if he plays basketball? We could start a church team."

"A lot of those New York teams were crooked."

"For what is man that Thou art mindful of him?" became his favorite text because as reply he could fill his sermons with stories of the great hardships and endurances of Vermonters. He loved the stories. The accounts of snow so deep a team of horses once rode level with the barn roof at Leland's. The story of old man Soames so crippled with arthritis last spring he had to crawl out on his hands and knees to strip the strawberries. Matthew West logging with one leg in plaster behind the same vicious team that crippled him. Stories of DeWit ("Do-It," they called him) Ferris, the third generation of Ferrises to run the feed and supply store, working night and day at two jobs because he was never able to stop making and losing his money on the horses, but faithfully and rightfully keeping the business in his son's name. Sunday mornings, placing Communion in their hands and against their parted lips, staring at their big teeth and long jaws, he felt a flow back to him through his wrists of their worth and merit.

"If you're going to keep on with this walking business, you better get it done before the snow flies," someone told him. He climbed the hills of the oldest farms, the ones that had been for generations in the same families. He looked up in library books the sites of Revolu-

The Calling

tionary houses and walked up side roads or even logging trails to see them all. He had bought himself a set of rough clothes from the Army-Navy store, and thick, yellow-tan hiking boots with crepe soles and long leather laces, and waterproofed them thoroughly with goose grease, and the stream's spray splattered on them and splattered on them as he stood dazzled by the rush of shallow, cold water, aware of the smell of freshness from it and the feel of cold air on his face, and everywhere, everywhere the changing fall leaves, a calliope of color above his head. "Oh who shall rest upon Thy holy hill," he decided he would begin next Sunday, joyful in his knowledge of the answer, "even he that leadeth an uncorrupt life."

"When's he going to talk about sin?"

"When's he going to talk about money?"

"We're the vestry, why can't we keep his Christmas bonus, Simmons?" one of them asked.

"He doesn't even know he's supposed to get one, so he wouldn't miss it."

"That's right, like Vesey says, you don't miss what you don't know about," said another.

"He isn't married, he doesn't need much money, Simmons."

"All he does is walk and collect things. He's got six, *six* old wagon wheels."

"What's he going to do? Open an antique shop?"

"If you don't give him his bonus," Simmons said, "how would you spend it?" with that little aspiriny smile of his when he knew he had won. They could agree to take the money, but never on how to spend an unbudgeted, unprecedented sum. In the end they had to decide to give the Christmas bonus to him, and Simmons was pleased. Simmons was protecting him, saving him, keeping him apart and watching him so he, Simmons, could be the one to tell him bit by bit, a little at a time, about the wrong in each good thing he found.

He was completely unprepared, Christmas morning, for the bonus Vesey gave him for the vestry, and he dared not look at it, terrified of seeing the amount, but crushed it at once in his hand, crumpled and wrinkled, jabbed into the pocket above his stupid, pounding heart.

He had Christmas dinner at Simmons's, listening to talk shouted over the TV, holding the youngest grandchild on his knee, admiring the huge, fresh-cut tree.

"Lots have aluminum nowadays," Simmons yelled at him.

"This one's a beauty," he answered.

"I'm scared of getting shocked by aluminum," Simmons said.

He burst out laughing. "Come on, Simmons, admit you like an honest tree."

"Walk out with me?" Simmons asked.

He agreed, and handed the child over to a woman. Simmons gave him his coat and boots, and they bundled up and burst out of the heat and uproar and smell of food inside the house into the flat, silent cold, their bodies shrunken by it and the air freezing their nostrils shut. "Oh," he gasped. He had stumbled from the hidden sidewalk into deep snow. "My damn boots are never high enough. How do you always manage? How many inches of snow do you get? This is fantastic. Look at it, Simmons. Stop a minute and look. What's more beautiful, the trees or the snow? If my life depended on it, I couldn't tell you which was more beautiful."

"They want you to help raise money for a new furnace in the church," Simmons said.

"That's great. We can use one. Why don't we make it?"

"Make it? You're a wonder, a true wonder. Out of what?"

"We've got everything we need, and the skills. Asa could do it by himself."

"Asa?"

"Asa Turner, sure."

"Take my advice. Don't go getting in with Asa."

"But he's the church caretaker."

"Never mind that. And the vestry isn't interested in handmade anything. They want a campaign, and fund-raising programs, and ads, and above all an organization that has positions with titles for all of them. A little of the big time. The fanciest and biggest church furnace campaign in the state."

The Calling

"That's silly. This is a simple little country church."
"Sure. That's why. They want to feel big."

"What's he think we hired him for?" Vesey said, then the others on the vestry began talking.

"He said he'd give us his bonus for the furnace," one said.

"I hope you took it," Blakeless said.

"Simmons there made me say no. It's like Simmons says, we don't want his bonus towards the furnace, we want a fund-raising campaign. Cities are supposed to do this all the time. He ought to know how to do it, but what he wants is to have more candlelight services. Hell, he'll shut off the electricity if we don't watch him."

"Simmons, you've got to talk to him. I tried at dinner last Friday. All he wanted to do was talk to my father-in-law about covered bridges and how to make dry-rock walls."

"What's he think we are? Fossils?"

"My, what fancy words you use, Damon."

"Can it, Simmons. You're so smart, you tell him what we want of a minister. And tell him about Asa."

"Asa?"

"Yeah, he's been logging with Asa. Next thing you know he'll get himself a hard hat and start taking off sugar and we'll begin having quilting bees in the church. You set him straight, Simmons. Tell him we want to raise money and do the church up right and not have any of this made-over antique stuff that never works. Asa's been getting him interested in that. You better tell him about Asa."

"That's right," Vesey said, "the truth never hurt anyone."

"If it doesn't hurt," Simmons said with satisfaction, "it's not the truth."

He had gone logging with Asa Turner. He stumbled up the hill, his breath rasping like a chain saw in and out of his lungs, or he half-slid, half-fell down the other side, clutching at branches to keep from sliding all the way. There was no flat land, it was all up or down, and everything was seen over the stream of his own gasping, frosted breath. There were no leaves left on the trees except for the evergreens, yet even here there were a dozen different shades of green. He had discovered the greens had different textures. There was a thick, prickly green in the spruce, dense and hard; and a light, soft, pliant green in pines, very feathery; and the red-based, rough-surfaced green of fir. He crushed a branch end of spruce in his hand to get the smell of resin, and the stiff broken spikes jabbed into his mittens. "This tree's got hold of me," he yelled out, pleased. "I need better gloves, Asa, like yours." Christ in heaven, how he loved it here. "Asa, wait. Let me lead the team some, Asa. Listen, listen, Asa, how much do you think these trees here are worth by the board foot, Asa?"

"No, the bonus is yours," Simmons told him. "They're touched by your trying to give it to them," he said with a funny, private smile, "but it's yours."

Simmons had taken him out to lunch. Not lobster, nor clam chowder, nothing New England, but the dullest place Simmons could think of: hamburger and chili sauce at a square cafe where the waitress knew everyone but refused to speak and silently placed the thick beige plates and the plastic glasses of un-iced water on the fake maple table that was still damp from her casual, sloshing cloth.

"They want a fund-raising campaign," Simmons said. "An up-to-date campaign. With advertising, and teams, and captains. They don't want anything to do with anything old unless they can sell it to tourists."

"They're beautiful. They work hard and believe in work. They never complain. They wouldn't know how to whine. Look at the fantastic stone walls, one stone at a time. And they still do it."

"Wainscott and his son you mean," Simmons said. "I knew you'd been visiting out there. They make them, sure, but they do it to get more money from tourists."

"Any tourist is lucky to get to come here."

Simmons watched him pouring bright red chili sauce on his hamburger.

"We could log the woods on church land and make money for a furnace," he said.

"Who you been with? Asa?"

"It would pay us a lot."

"Crap. Asa's ideas of finance. He'll want a hundred of us to go out and split rails to pay taxes next."

"He's the strongest man I've ever seen. He doesn't even mind the cold. I've seen him out in a wool shirt and no coat or sweater even, at sixteen degrees, and his hands weren't even cold."

"Did he tell you he'd been in prison?" Simmons asked.

"Yes, Simmons. He did. The second time I talked to him, if you want to know. I grew up around more men who'd been in prison, or should have been, than you've got in this state."

"Did he tell you why he was in prison?" Simmons pushed him.

"I don't care."

"He raped his thirteen-year-old stepdaughter. Lots of times. His wife was in the hospital having another baby and with some sort of trouble over it, so he was taking the kid to bed nights. She said it at school, said her stomach hurt her. That's how they found out. The school nurse caught on. Some people say she's not Asa's stepdaughter but one of his own. Plenty of incest with those Turners. You can't tell any of the kids apart they look so much alike. Inbred stock the lot of them. All those same ears. You ever notice their ears? They've got ears thick as cups and pretty near the same shape."

"What happened to her?"

"Who?" Simmons said.

"The stepdaughter."

"Her. Oh, she was found a place somewhere. Some kind of school or something. A state place, I think."

"You mean she was sent away?"

"That's right."

"Away from here and everyone she knows?"

"You bet. Got her right away. Best thing to do."

"I don't agree. I absolutely don't agree."

"You don't know the Turners. Or what was being said about the girl. Seen bees come around new-spilt honey?" Simmons said.

"It was wrong. They shouldn't have done it," he said. "They shouldn't have been allowed to send her away from here and her home. Did you know about it? Did other members of the church? Why didn't they help her? How could all of you know about it and let a thing like that happen?"

"Well, you know too, now, don't you?"

For a minute there was quiet.

"And you know I do, right?" he said.

"Why, that's so too," Simmons said, "that's so too."

"He's the first minister I ever liked," Simmons said.

"The city sure teaches them how to use the phone. He's spent two days on the phone. He knows how to get things done on it."

"Who's paying?"

"Relax, Blakeless. The calls weren't made from the church. Ruthanne told me so 'cause she put them through for him."

"Why's he so interested in that Turner girl, Simmons?"

"I don't think the girl's much, she's just the worm in the apple, you might say," Simmons said.

"All the same, he went to see her. And what's more, he took Asa."

"Asa?" Simmons said.

"I did it," waving clasped hands over his head, "I did it. I knew something Simmons didn't. Yeah, he went to Burlington with Asa yesterday morning."

"Well, the sly, sly fox," Simmons said. "The sly old fox." Simmons began to chuckle, pleased, softly, not to anyone except himself, and said again, aloud, "The sly, sly fox."

"What'd Asa say about it?" Vesey asked.

"You know Asa. He'll talk a thousand hours about horses or trees or the weather, but never what you want to talk about. He always said it was no rape, anyway. Said she was willing enough."

"You know those Turners."

"There'll be a line of the men waiting to see that girl, I bet."

"Can he make them let her go up at Burlington?" one asked.

"He's the minister, he can fix it," Damon said.

"He's got nerve, taking Asa over there. How'd he manage that?"

"Hell. Like Damon says, he's the minister isn't he?"

"And so he is, now," Simmons said. "Listen to all of you—respecting him."

"What's he going to do with her? Put her with kin?"

"He didn't say. He's doing it all himself, and saying nothing to anyone."

"Well, well," Simmons said, "well, well."

He had forgotten about his gloves again and ripped a half-inch of skin from three fingers that touched the car handle. He went into Simmons's for a bandage and Simmons himself put on a yellow salve and wrapped the fingers.

"Fantastic cold," he said. "How can they log in this kind of weather? I understand the trees freeze solid and then snap with enormous force when they're cut and the danger of being hurt comes from that. What's the deepest snow you remember?"

"Don't recall. That hand'll be sore."

"I keep forgetting about metal. What do I owe you?"

"Nothing, nothing," Simmons said. "I hear you've been traveling a bit? How was the trip?"

"Informative. It's great to be home. The air's so good here."

"You going to get that girl out?"

"I am."

"McManus said you bought a whole outfit of clothes for her at his store. Must have spent your whole bonus on it, didn't you? I thought so. Said you'd got her size for everything."

"She comes home Wednesday. Her aunt and I are bringing her."

"Her aunt?"

"No more gossip, Simmons. Her aunt. Asa's youngest sister."

"Asa's?"

"Yes, Asa's, damn it. Her own people."

"'I am the resurrection and the life,'" he cried out loudly so they could hear him as he came from the little side room following the coffin into the church for Asa's stepdaughter's funeral. Rachel, it turned out her name was. She had hanged herself in the loft of the old barn, climbing up into it and because the loft was low having to center the rope above the open stairway, but even so her legs could not stretch out full, and they had to cut her down and carry her into the house and let her thaw before her knees and ankles could be laid out natural and straight. "'He that believeth in me shall never die,'" he read.

    The church had only Turners in it. Identical faces gazing up at him like rows of round-eared cows. There were no men at the service, only women, except for a male child or two in the multi-littered families. A baby sucking a bottle could have been male. What could he say to them to help them and not only himself? All they had talked about when he visited the house was that she had gone out to the barn barefoot. And how on earth had she remembered about that loft? And what a shame when she had those new clothes. And how froze her feet had been.

    Simmons had driven him out to the house. Simmons would not go inside but sat in the car, and one after another the Turner men went out and stood in the freezing air chatting through the car window and over the sound of the engine running to keep it warm. In the house he talked to the women. There was no question of his comforting them. They were garrulous and loud and spirited, two or three talking at once always, and a child rolling unclothed and untended under the kitchen stove for warmth. That she was barefoot was what they talked about. That she had gone out to the barn without even any socks on, and that her feet were blue.

    What could he say from his prayer book any better than that? "Lord, make me not a rebuke unto the foolish . . . for I am a stranger with thee, a sojourner . . ."? That was in the burial service. And, "Oh spare me a little, that I may recover my strength, before I go hence, and be no more seen"?

    Sunday he did not come in as the minister should do behind his processing choir. The congregation stirred looking for him. He came from the side room, walking quickly and with his head down. He wore no cleric's white collar, no surplice, no robe. He climbed straight into the pulpit without any prefatory prayer or benediction. A rustle of uneasiness went through his parishioners, a widespread turning of heads and flurry of tiny, checking glances and sniffing dilation of nostrils, all in the way of horses penned by the approach of an unseen but dreaded fire. He bent forward, gripping the pulpit's edge as he always did, his hands curled onto each side.

"Romans thirteen, verse eight," he began, far too loud, his voice grinding dead in his throat. "Romans thirteen, verse eight," he began again. "'Owe no man anything but to love one another, for he that loveth another hath fulfilled the law.'"

"Some men," he began, still too loud, and then tried once more, "some men do good when they love." In the fourth row Simmons ripped the glasses from his face and shielded them on his knee, his palms pressed over the lenses as a child covers his ears against unbearable sounds. "Some men have a faith that helps others, and gives others faith, and makes them happier and, sometimes, better. Some men do no harm where they go. They cause no hurt to those whom they try to help. They do not make other men worse. They do not make them mean or cruel, but bigger than they were, and kinder, and, and sometimes, more Christian. Some men do add to good when they find it. Once, long ago. . . . Once, I. . . . Once. . . ."

He slipped slowly down the side of the pulpit as if it had come over him that his only problem was that he could not stand any longer, and with slow relief his knees gave way and he sat, half sideways, on the narrow chair reserved for setting his books and papers on, or a glass of water, hand still on the pulpit and head nodding from side to side with the light and flexible ease of a long-stemmed flower pulled up in a child's playful fist. The murmuring of the congregation and the choir behind him seemed only to soothe him, and his head rocked from side to side, from side to side until at last he let go of the pulpit and laid his face forward in the shallow skin-and-bone cradle of his hands.

Simmons was on his feet, glasses clutched in his hand and his eyes squinted to make out shapes, bursting out at once into the only hymn upon which he had any solid claim of memory:

"'Onward, Christian so-o-ol-diers,'" he sang in full voice, and with one shuffle the congregation rose jubilantly—freed, exuberant with relief—joyously taking up the call in grateful, roaring unison, "'marching as to-o war. . . .'"

Beginnings

She went away and grew up.

When she came back they all recognized her, but no one knew who she was.

"Don't tell me," they cried. "Now don't tell. I know, I know, sure, Claudine, or Murphetta. One of them anyway, aren't you? Of course you are, I'd know you anywhere. You haven't changed a bit."

She held her books or poems, her paintings or reviews about her, before her as a talisman. And a reminder.

"I'm only home for a visit," she said. She did not talk the way they did anymore, which is what they meant when they grinned and nodded and peppered one another on the cheeks with little sideways glances brimming like popcorn out of the rims of their eyes.

They didn't like her clothes, her earrings, the tossing of her hair, but she and they knew why she sported them, loud in the streets, loud in the living rooms, loud in the wings of other people's talk.

For where is fame any good except at home? What "oh's" and "ah's" matter except those from the lips that have smacked open and shut over the first twelve, or twenty, years?

"Here's applesauce the way you like it. Rich in cloves and sicky sweet. I never understood myself how you could eat it, but I bet you didn't get any of that where you were?"

"No."

And then of course the walk with an accompanying person. Past the school (where for the first and last time tears had come beneath a smiling adult's causing), past the play-yard shrubs whose bark, whose juicy taste, her mouth remembered on its own and reworked as she went by. Past the fountain that had never any water. The aim of her journey to come by a slow encircling upon that spot (a half-lot of shady trees), or building (a gargoyle of a house), or person (the librarian, perhaps, or the owner of a jewelry store) in whose presence first she knew, *knew,* that she was meant, *she, meant,* to write, paint, sing . . . whatever it was.

"Why are you going this way?" her companion said. "There's nothing here. This part of town's all run down now. To see the valley? Can you see the valley from here? Oh, between those two houses? Why, so you can. What do you know about that. Where are you going now? Back there? Behind that building . . . why? Wait . . . wait . . . say, you're right, there is a stained-glass window in the attic of that house. Why, you remember things no one even knows. Would it surprise you to hear I didn't know this place existed?"

"No."

"Why did you come back here anyway? *I* wouldn't if I could get out of this dump. There's nothing here to see or do. You wouldn't catch me coming back here if I could get away."

"Oh," she was saying, "where? . . where? . . how? . . ." has that half-lot of trees gone, she meant, or that old building, or that special person.

"Uprooted, torn down; fired, or died," she was told. "Years ago."

Where was her starting point, then? Where was she to lay, or to display, the first symbolic copy, print, review? Where did she think she was?

She sat beside her childhood's table on her childhood's narrow bed (under a roof, sloped or square, high or low) and pondered. Self-confident, disciplined, alive . . . yes, *yes,* she was. Then what insanity had brought her here—she who knew better, whose knowing was in her work—expecting any other. Applesauce rich in cloves and sugar, indeed. How possibly anything else? Idiot.

Packing was swift, for the real storage had been done long ago.

"Off?" they said. "So soon?" they said. "Well, don't forget us," they said.

"I won't. I won't. I never will," said Claudine, or Murphetta, and hitching her books, her poems, her paintings, or her reviews up under her arm, she left, as before, through a golden door.

Consider the Lily

"Her room was always full of flowers," I said. "Shelves and tables covered with them, and half the time we didn't even know who sent them."

"All the same," Jay answered, "she'd be remembered more if Alexander were a better-known poet. Or more to the point, as well known as he should be."

"I don't care," I said. "He never really wrote about her anyway, just about himself—his yearning, his regret, his love, his grief. How he felt about the way she changed. Never about her."

"Still, it's how most people come to know of her now, isn't it?"

"Yes. All right, yes, I suppose so," I said.

We were speaking of my mother, of course, and this was the first time I had admitted Jay was right, and that knowledge of her did in any way depend on Alexander. I could not help but admit it. It was true that separate from Alexander she was being forgotten, and the vivid picture of her that people once carried in their minds was fading. How long, after all, had it been, longer than I could remember, since anyone had greeted me with the once-common, awed, "You're Andrea Croft's daughter? Honestly?" Part of which, I agree, may have been sheer surprise, for we weren't look-alikes, Andrea and I. One old gentleman even asked me, in that first flush of shock, if I had been adopted. He was not meaning to be cruel, I could see that, but was just not able to tolerate this blemish on his vision of Andrea.

It was not that I was so ugly, or so plain, but that Andrea was so beautiful. Truly beautiful. The sort of beauty that flew out at you, and you never got used to it, never stopped staring at her, in hidden ways, when you were with her. Even years after she was dead, when a friend asked me what I remembered most about my mother, the first thing I said was, "Her beauty." "How sad for you," was the reply, "your own mother." "Nonsense," I disagreed, "nonsense."

At least let me have the pleasure of her beauty now, since it caused us enough trouble and came enough between us then. Just as, in another way, it made no difference at all. Or so I thought. It is hard for me to know the truth about it. Things get muddled, and I am not so sure, now, what happened to us and what we felt, and what people just said happened and wrote that we felt. I came to hate so much the magazine version of us as "Famous Beauty and Her Daughter, Pity Them Both," that I wonder if I did not overlook the truth that was in it. For the very fact that there was such a view did influence us. It was because of it, after all, that Andrea sent me off to school when both of us would have preferred to stay together. We had no one else. Not at that time, anyway.

I was Andrea's only child. My father had left us, left Andrea, when I was three. I was too young to know why, and when I was old enough to ask, Andrea seemed to have no clear explanation, or would not give me one. I think now that she, too, probably was not sure why. I saw my father frequently. When I was eleven he married again, to a kind woman a few years older than himself. She wanted very much to take me into her home and be a mother to me. She was sure Andrea was a dreadful, wicked, arrogant woman and bad for me. I never openly argued with her. I think I sensed, even at my age, that it meant a great deal to her to feel she had saved my father from "that woman." She had to have something, I thought, to hold against that beauty. And my father was happy with her. But I never did go to live with them.

Andrea did ask me once if I wanted to stay longer on visits to my father. That must have been around the time she was beginning to have this notion, caught from gossip or magazine stories or from the free advice she was always getting, that she was a bad influence on me. Someone had discussed it with her, probably. People were always doing that, discussing her life with her and her feelings. "What is it like to be so beautiful?" I heard one woman ask. And then wait there for an answer, as if Andrea had to tell. As if her beauty and her fame gave a passport to her privacy. Andrea never minded much. And sometimes what they said made her laugh. But when anyone spoke of me, it was different. She could not be so sure when they spoke about me, and since it was true that she was beautiful and I was not, was it not also true that she was harming me?

She began taking me out more. She began to worry when I stayed alone and invited few friends to my home. But we had never led that sort of life. And every effort she made to move me into a wider circle of companions brought her more attention and made me more than ever simply a handy built-in all-purpose audience and admirer for her. When a picture of both of us, the two of us together, appeared full-page in a Sunday supplement, she decided to send me away to school.

Yet the funny thing was, I was truly not unhappy. I was not made miserable. I loved Andrea. She was my mother. I liked being with her, and I liked our life in New York. I even liked her modeling sessions with photographers, the public appearances, the general excitement around her. I did not think of myself as pathetic, and I did not want to go off to some dull school in the country full of silly people my own age. I did not want to leave Andrea, and what's more (better?) I knew she did not want to send me away. I was nearly seventeen then, and I was becoming a good friend for her. We got on very well, and there was no one else for her. Not then, anyway.

All the same, Andrea was determined that I should go off for my last year of high school. Between us we picked a school, and even chose a likely college for the following year. Andrea pulled strings at the school, for we were applying late, and I was admitted. So it was done, and we had three months of the summer left for ourselves. We spent almost all of the time together. I went with Andrea to all her modeling appointments and kept notes for her about them. Afterwards we would have lunch or supper together in whatever restaurant caught my eye. This was the summer before she had made many movies, but even so she was becoming known around the City. We always got a special table no matter how crowded it was. And it never mattered what she was wearing or how she was dressed, the maitre d' always held her chair and ordered for her. Lord, she was beautiful the summer before I left!

Then it was time for me to pack. Because Andrea was working so many hours in the day, we ended up doing the packing late into the night and were edgy with each other. She got angry because I was so untidy. She started giving me a long lecture, telling me I must do better when I was away, telling me there would be no one at school to pick up after me, or take care of my clothes, or tidy my drawers. Or clean my hairbrush for me.

"Look at it," she said, picking out my hairbrush from the clutter on my bureau. "You can't brush your hair with it like this, all matted up. Might as well rub your head with a brick. You should clean the bristles every time. Don't you know that?" and she began tugging the hairs free, jerking and pulling them with short quick movements of her fingers.

"I don't know," she said, "what I am going to do without you, when you're gone."

I sat quite still on my bed, and she kept on pulling out hairs from my brush. "But I want to do the right thing for you," she said. "More than anything else, I want to do what is best for you."

As if the one guaranteed best thing would be to send me away from her, get me out of her presence. For she had become the shadow in which I lived. Or was I her shadow following everywhere behind her? Either way, that was how much the myth about us had got to her. And to me too; yes, to me too. We both read those newspapers and the stories in those magazines.

"I want you to have what other girls have," Andrea was saying, and something more about what she wanted for me, but I could not pay attention. I kept being disconcerted because she had put the brush down and there were strands of my hair, brown, not black like hers, being stretched and twisted in her fingers.

"Damn," she said, rolling my hair into a ball. "I suppose if I'd had smallpox it would all be fine and you could stay at home and go to school like other girls." Said bitterly, and I had a strange, loosening feeling as she said it. I felt something come unwound inside me.

"Even if you'd had smallpox," I said, "I'd have to go out on my own sometime. Even if we swapped faces," and it was good to say it out loud just once. We had never spoken of it. "Even if I were beautiful," I said, "I would still have to leave the old nest."

"Yes. Yes, you would, wouldn't you?"

"Sure. And anyway, it isn't as if it bothered us any," I said. "It's never made any real difference to us, to you and me," I said. Oh I felt adult—my first deliberate and unselfish lie for someone else. I was really very young, even for my age. What on earth, I wonder now, did Andrea feel about my small stiff lie? Amusement, perhaps. Amusement (and love?), as she stood there looking at me over the piles of clothes we had yet to pack.

"What would it have been like," I asked Jay, "if cameras had never been invented?"

"I've read that crowds would line the streets and people stand on chairs at balls to catch a glimpse of the great Victorian beauties," he said.

"And some of them had families," I said, "and some of them must even have had daughters? That's what's in your head, right? But you're wrong, exactly wrong, if you believe Andrea thought of herself only as a great beauty. That was how she made our living. The rest Alexander made up so he could write about it."

"Some of it, maybe."

"Yes," I said. "Yes, look at these. Look how he wrote on the backs of photographs she chose as her best each year. And here, how he wrote alongside her own notes to herself on lighting and the safest camera angles. He loved all this—the beauty and then the fading beauty story—it became his myth. She and I both fought against it."

But the school Andrea and I chose turned out worse than I had expected. Everyone kept asking me about Andrea, and it was harder than being with her had ever been. I began to lose the sense of her as my mother. More and more she became simply the starting point for a flood of comments and questions, always the same—oh, look, there's a picture of Andrea Croft again, what's she like? does she look like that in person? what's it like to be close to her? what's she wear around the house?

"There she is, Andrea Croft, my old Mom," I'd yell out when we came on one of her pictures. I, who had never called her "Mom" in my life. "My old crafty Crofty Mom," I'd say, hinting it was all some trick she contrived, some fraud and I was in on it with her. I'd laugh loudly, carrying the others along with me, for though they were puzzled, I found out quickly enough that they were willing to join in the laughing about her. I hated myself for that, more even than I hated those glossy, gleaming, endlessly beautiful photographs.

Yet time does let us change. It turned out I was excellent at my school work. I could remember everything I read with virtually no effort, but none of that seemed to make much difference until about halfway through my first zoology course, when all at once, with simply no resistance, I fell into science like a stone into the sea. It was the lab work. Never in my life, not later in my career, not in marriage, not with any of my children, has there been a time of absorption more intense than those first hours in the basement lab. I felt the entire subject of zoology existed for me, and somehow the frog's veins and slippery layers of muscles were mine, so easily did I find and learn them. I spent the second half of that year in a daze of work and learning and happiness, all of it self-contained, newborn, as if the first breaths I had really deeply breathed were scented with formaldehyde.

When school ended, feeling vastly pleased with myself and my grades and eager for college, I began packing to go home. But time had moved on for Andrea, too. She had seen me at Thanksgiving and Christmas, of course. But now I could not quite make up my mind whether she was really working, as she told me, or whether she wanted me to have a longer break from her this important first year for me, as I chose to believe. For she sent me to my father's that summer. Later on, of course, I learned that it had nothing to do with me at all. She had gone to Scotland with Alexander. She did not want me around.

A few days before I was to go to college, Andrea came back to New York City and arranged for me to come down and see her. In one way, I had forgotten her. I had forgotten what it was like actually to see her. Like all the others, like anyone, I stopped and gawked. There was such beauty in her.

Then I had a sick feeling she was going to say something trite, something like the lines from those magazines in which her pictures appeared, or worse, like the dialogue in that bad movie she had made. But she did not. She nodded and nodded at me, approving and happy, and she said, "You've grown up so, Julie. You've grown up, and so nicely."

It's Mother, I thought, not even thinking I had ever used any other name for her. "Mother," I called her, as we hugged, and all that afternoon I could hear my voice using the word to her over and over. And I did all the talking—about school, about college, about my grades and how I had found out I could do anything they asked in a lab and what I was going to do and be. I talked and talked, and she listened, and fixed us sandwiches for supper, which we ate, standing in the kitchen, while I talked. Finally I said, "How about you? You look great, blooming. Better than ever."

She smiled. She was openly, but self-consciously, happy. Because of me, I thought. I swear I did, I thought it was because she was so proud of me. I was that naive. It never entered my head that she could look like that because of someone else.

•

"Suppose it is true," I said to Jay, "that mostly people do know of her now because of Alexander. He wasn't any good for her when she was alive. One of the hardest things for her all her life was the way her looks isolated her. He made that worse. He celebrated it. He wanted her to think of herself as 'the great and rare beauty.' Then she would fit into what he wrote. But she wasn't that way—not before. And she didn't like what he tried to do to her. How else can you explain that note he added in her copy of the poems he wrote about her?"

I meant the penciled lines "Oh Andrea, why *shouldn't* I love your beauty and write about your beauty and be grateful to you for your beauty? That's what it's for. Why not, for . . ." above his poem:

> Consider the Lily
> Whose white lips seal
> All answer to her beauty,
> Whose mute appeal
> Is but herself revealed,
> And from whose throat
> The only sound is beauty.
> Should I stand singing by
> Her layered petals 'til I grow
> Rooted, still
> I would not move a single person so.

"It makes no sense, his having written that note," I said, "unless she had complained."

"You aren't really going to tell me her looks came between them?" Jay asked.

"No, all right," I said, laughing. "Obviously not. But he wasn't good for her, Jay."

"On the contrary, I think she might have enjoyed being with someone who relished her beauty openly and honestly, someone who thought it was great and took it in his stride."

"In his stride my eye. He went into fits over her, behaving as if she were a shrine and he the head keeper. And then reading his poems about her in public after her death. It was disgusting."

"He loved her."

"You always say that. So what? A lot of people loved her. He was bad for her. He made her fake. She began behaving like some Hollywood movie queen starting to age. It was terrible. He did that. Alexander did. He made her that way—colder. Someone else."

Not that I saw her so much in those years, to try to be honest. I was busy with college and my studies, and it seemed perfectly natural to spend Christmas with visiting English cousins and the summer with my father and stepmother. By September, Andrea was on the Coast making a movie, and I went back to college without seeing her at all, although we talked often on the phone. My sophomore year of college began. I was doing well. I even had a small job as a lab assistant. I was happy.

Consider the Lily

One evening, for no reason I can remember, it hit me that I had not seen Andrea in over a year. And that I seldom wrote to her. I couldn't even remember when I had written her last, or what I had said to her. I told her less and less about myself, and nothing at all about my friends. Not even that I had any. All right, so what? There was more. I avoided any movie if she was in it. I would not look at magazines in which she was likely to appear, and I would not read articles about her. I never talked about her in college. So? Go on, go on, there was still more. All right, there were people, a lot of people, who? all right, some of my teachers, all right, even my zoology lab instructor, who did not know she was my mother. Because I had carefully not told them. The book I was reading, a textbook, heavy, thick, scored and underlined, a comfortable weight in my hands, slid down onto my stomach. I could no longer concentrate on it.

I went downstairs and into one of the phone booths, and dropped coins in, dialed her number, and waited. Opposite me, through the glass, I could see the tiers of mailboxes, a honeycomb of wood, some of the niches filled and many not. Automatically I glanced at mine. I always did, always looked, though no one wrote me regularly except Andrea.

The phone rang and rang. She isn't going to answer, I thought. Then she did.

"Mother? It's me. Julie. I called to say hello."

"Why, how nice. How very nice of you."

"I hadn't seen you in a while . . . a long time. I just realized it."

"Are you well, darling? It's lovely to hear you. You're sure you're well?"

"Oh sure, absolutely sure."

I was beginning to sweat. A dampness on my hands. It spread onto the black phone where I was holding it.

"Are you liking it there, darling? You're getting on with everyone? Darling? Are you making friends? You never say."

"Oh yes, sure." I was not listening to her. "I was thinking though," I said, "I mean, I thought . . . that is, I just thought I'd like to see you."

"I'd like that too. Why don't you come in to the City?"

"I was thinking," I said, and I was holding tight to the slick phone for support, "I was thinking, why don't you come here?

There's something they call Parents Day. Payment Day, the kids call it. Because they hit parents for contributions. Lots of parents come. You never have. I'd like you to see it. I'd like you to meet some of the kids and my teachers." I shut my eyes. "And I'd like to have them meet you."

For a second she did not answer. I sat, holding the phone loosely. I was in no rush now. I felt cleaned out and suddenly sleepy, the way you do after you've been good and sick and thrown up everything.

"Yes," Andrea said, "I can come. Yes."

I liked the way she did not ask if I were sure I really wanted her and did not go on and on testing me, but just said "Yes."

Probably the college's biggest event in a decade was Andrea Croft's visit. She was very famous by then. She both swamped and made that Parents Day. Everyone tried to be casual and cool with her, and of course could not. I did not care. I wanted them to gape and point and whisper. She deserved it. I took her to everything and introduced her to every single person I knew. I think she enjoyed it, too. I took her in to the fancy smorgasbord lunch in the Hall. That is what you did with your parents on Parents Day. It's funny, I remember thinking, but she isn't dressed so differently from anyone else, and yet even as we came in the door, even as we entered, people began turning toward her. She had an aura around her, I swear she did. No one could keep from looking at her.

I picked a big table for us, so there would be room for everyone. All the college kids I knew and the faculty and the dormitory staff began coming over. And finally our President did. He was a distinguished, acid-tongued man, with tight laugh lines around his mouth. Very self-possessed. Yet I saw him stumble once between his words from staring at her. I knew just how he felt. Alexander wrote some lines about it that described it perfectly. Perfectly.

> I am no match for the distance between her eyes.
> Paradise, perhaps, has some such measurement,
> Men here do not;
> Nor does a spring or waterfall
> Fix fathoms for that mindfall of surprise
> That those whom she has looked upon

> Are lost to common lives,
> Having walked weightless once
> In that infinity between her wide-spaced eyes.

Andrea began deliberately to charm the President, with time out for one quick conspiratorial glance at me. For the first time (and I admit I was shocked) I saw the fun there was for her, as well, in all this beauty business.

When the President left her I went with two other students to fetch coffee for our table. Coming back I heard someone ask her, "And which one is your daughter?" and she answered, "Why, good heavens, that one; why Julie, of course." It is a sentence I love to remember.

After that Parents Day I saw Andrea more often, though not usually for more than a day or two and sometimes for only a few hours. I was sure, by my junior year, that I wanted to go on into graduate work in zoology, and she and I spent hours talking about where I should go to study and how we would arrange it. And we worked together to find lab jobs for me in the summer. We had good, brief times together. And once we quarreled.

We were at Andrea's cottage at the beach, and we had done too much sunbathing and were both burned, though she not so badly as I. We stood looking each other over in the bathroom.

"You don't even burn," I said, looking at her back. "It isn't fair. And you're the picture of youth. You never grow old."

"Yes I do. You don't look closely enough."

"Where? I don't believe it. Where?" I was instantly alert. I wanted to see. "Where?"

"Oh, the neck. That's the traditional first place. All over the neck." She was not pleased.

Yet I could not resist moving closer and examining her carefully in the hard bathroom light. Then I said, "Oh, not much. Not really much, just a little." I quelled the urge, with my hand raised, to touch her skin where it was showing age. Other people get to touch their mothers, I thought angrily.

"I'll get us some sunburn lotion," I said instead. I pulled open one of the cabinets. It was crammed with cosmetics. The sort I thought she never used. I had not even known there were that many brands and kinds you could buy. She had never used them before. Professional makeup, yes, but not all this.

"For heaven's sake," I said.

"The sun lotion's over to the right," she said. "In the plastic bottle. Here. I'll get it. You're so messy. You can never find anything."

"But you never used to keep all this glop. What's it for?"

"Guess."

"You don't mind getting old, older, do you? What do a few lines matter?"

No reply. She was looking down and opening the sunburn lotion.

"Do you really mind?" I could not help my voice sounding excited, even gay.

"No," she said. And then, "Yes, I do. Why shouldn't I mind? Of course I mind. It would be absurd to change now. I'm used to being the way I am. It's shaped my life. I've had to give up enough because of my looks, it would be absurd to lose them now."

"What?" I said. "What have you given up?" pouncing on those words. You, I wanted her to say. You, my daughter, you all these years, you.

"Oh, this and that. It doesn't matter," she said. "I don't see why it's so strange that I shouldn't want to grow old. It's a natural reaction."

"I want to know what you gave up," I said. She was holding out the bottle of lotion to me but I brushed it aside. "I'm not a child. Don't bring things up and then cut me off," I said.

"Cut you off? How?"

"You began it," I told her. "You started talking about what you've given up. All right then, tell me what. What *did* you give up that mattered to you? What . . . or who?" There, I had almost finished the sentence for her, so much did I want her to say the words, so much did I want to hear them. Why wouldn't she?

"You have no right to talk to me like that," she said angrily, "just because I'm your mother. You're touchy; well, so am I. You have no right to pry. I have feelings too."

I was stunned, and furious. I had no idea what we were quarreling about, but I was outraged with her and her unfairness. I would not answer her. Andrea squeezed the bottle of lotion and told me coldly to turn around so she could coat my back. Without saying a word, I did. And in the same mood we finished out the day. We were still angry even when we parted, and I took the train back to college.

Andrea wrote to me at once. A pleasant, friendly letter with no mention of that day. I deliberately let the time drift by without answering. I must have been, I suppose, really very hurt.

Then in April I read in a newspaper that she was ill in the City. In terror I fled to New York, convinced she would be dead before I got to her. She was sitting up in her hospital room and was delighted to see me, and terribly amused at my panic because she knew exactly how I felt and why. We both laughed at my guilty haste, so childish and so understandable. It entertained her enormously, and she kept going back to it. I had come in such a rush I had packed nothing and even needed to borrow clothes from her for the night. This, too, entertained her. I loved to hear her laugh.

She never mentioned and I did not say, though I had read about it in the same newspaper story, that Alexander was in Scotland. I stayed with her in the hospital all the next day, too. We talked and tried to play cards, but she could not focus on their faces. And she could not read.

I sat in the armchair beside her and in the hours that she slept, I looked at her. We were happy the whole day. It was the last time. Three days later she was dead.

We tried—her agent, my father and I, an English cousin, Alexander's nephew, Jay—to keep her funeral private. It was not possible. Too many people felt they owed her . . . no, I meant to say *owned* her. Well, whatever, they came.

Afterwards, it was expected that I would take care of Andrea's personal belongings. But they were all mixed together with stacks of Alexander's books and papers. It turned out he worked most in her New York apartment. I had not met him before and would not now. Someone (perhaps Jay himself) suggested that Jay, since he was not only Alexander's nephew and his friend but also his lawyer, help me sort the books and papers and take the ones belonging to Alexander.

It was not that easy. In her apartment he wrote, it seemed, on every surface a pencil could mark: his work journals and papers and drafts of poems, of course; but also on the backs of prints of her pictures, in her appointment books, down the sides of her own notes on each photographer with whom she worked. I insisted on reading everything—even the pages from Alexander's letters, never finished or never mailed. I read and read them. Some I know by heart:

> Last night she was sewing. She, sewing. So long as I could make myself, until my teeth ground on each other, I stood watching. Then I went to her, took all those threads and needles out of her hands. And did what I have wanted, ached to do since I first saw her, before I saw her, since I saw pictures of her, before that, since I saw pictures of Greek sculpture, since I ever saw a single perfect thing.
>
> "Let me," I said, "let me," and put my hands over her eyes, covering her eyes. She closed them as I did. I felt them close. "No," I whispered, "look at me," and felt beneath my palms the brush of her eyelashes as she opened her eyes. I held my breath, then moved my hands aside to hold her face. And she was looking at me.
>
> I did not die of it.
>
> Strange that sleeping she looks blind. Statue-like. The eyes too widely spaced, perhaps. There is an intense immobility about her face asleep. An eternal immobility, as from first principles always known— that yes yes yes quality of beauty. And the eyes beautiful even in sleep, even seeming blind. The very shape of them in her face. I am terrified that she will open them suddenly and look on me. And yet I want her to. Would I be slain? I ask you, what happens when the rose looks back? I go in when she is sleeping. I go in like a kid, with my heart pounding in my ears.

"Surely you knew about your mother and Alexander," Jay finally asked me as we sat before those papers.

"Not like this."

"Didn't you see them together? Well, you must have read about them? It was all over the newspapers."

"Oh yes," I said. It was mostly a lie. I could not make myself say that I never read anything about Andrea except the bare headlines that crashed through my barriers. Had she, too, assumed I had read the stories about them? "I'm interested in different things," I said primly. "I'm going to be a zoologist."

"That's fine. Fine," Jay said. "But you must have known they were together?"

I said nothing.

"At least you know who he is, don't you?"

"Yes. I thought he'd quit writing poetry."

"He had, until he met her. Don't you see?"

"These are horrible," I said. "These poems about her getting old and about each new wrinkle and how aged she looked in certain lights. Like studying a china doll cracking, not a person. I hate these; they're indecent."

"Here," Jay said, and took them from me, and I remember saying to him, "I didn't know poetry was written this way, all in bits and pieces scrawled on anything."

"Sometimes, maybe, it starts that way," Jay said, and he put the whole collection aside. "We don't have to do this now," he said. Alexander, he went on to tell me, had gone back to the island in Scotland where they had stayed. There was no rush.

So I let the separating be. Jay came at intervals over time and took away the books and letters and the work journals belonging entirely to Alexander. As for Andrea's papers, they, like her flowers, concerned so many people I did not even know. Yet many of the papers, too, were mine—my letters to her, my report cards, my themes, my college papers, my early lab reports. There were her own diaries, of course. They were filled with professional appointments and comments and advice to herself about different photographers and agencies. In the midst of just such an entry was a line about me: "Last night Sheila T. said I talked all the time about Julie and bragged all the time about Julie, and Alexander told her to shut up." I read that over and over, that one entry in her clear, square handwriting.

And the page about our quarrel, that summer we were sunburned. She had written:

> Tonight I quarreled w. Julie and let her go back to school w. both of us angry. Foolish, but so typical. What she wants is for me not to be beautiful. It is what they all want, most of them. They think there is

some real me hidden somewhere else, separate from the beauty, separate from the way I look. But there is no other me. And what they don't know is that it is the beauty they want anyway, not the hidden me. Even Julie. She thinks she wants a mother, but she has had one and hasn't noticed because of trying to catch at the beauty, which she wants even more, or wants to use, perhaps, as A. does so freely and joyfully. Yet I have loved her need of it, as on Parents Day when she asked me to come to her college to help her make friends because she had not made any on her own. I loved helping her, no matter what part of me was doing the helping.

That was what she thought. However many times I read it, I could not believe it. That was what she thought. She had not known me at all, nor I her. It was a wonder we even knew each other's names. It was a wonder that when she called "Julie," it was I who came. And yet I did. And we did love each other, I swear we did.

"You musn't become obsessed by her," Jay said.
"I'm not," I said. "I'm not obsessed."
"Nor by your myth, as you would call it, of her either," Jay said.
"But I'm not. How could I be?"
Though it is true that sometimes, unexpectedly, I remember the way she looked. I remember the way she tipped her head and there would be a valley there beneath her cheekbone. A valley. Alexander called it that. Until her death, until I read what he had written, I had no way to say what I had been seeing in her face.

"Tell me about Alexander," I asked Jay.
"Why didn't you let him meet you?" Jay asked. He was still angry about it. "You never saw him."
I did not answer. The truth was, I had seen Alexander. One time. At a memorial service for Andrea three weeks after she died. I knew at once who he was. He was tall and heavy-boned, with big, yellow teeth and stiff hair. I had thought, instantly, my God, no wonder he loved her. But I refused to meet him.

"No, but tell me," I insisted, "what was he like?"
"Tall. Six three or more when he didn't slouch. He looked more like a logger than a New Jersey poet. He'd done everything. He'd been a waiter, a singer, worked on ranches, been in and out of

schools all over Europe. He once sharpened knives in the Bronx for a living. Then he settled to full-time writing, and some teaching and editing a review. He'd stopped writing any poetry for years before he met Andrea."

"Yes."

"He began again after he met her."

"He fed on her. That's all he wanted out of her, to use her. His muse."

"Have you ever thought what her life would have been like if she hadn't met him? You were away at school then. She had few friends she liked, you've told me that yourself, and many of them truly were sycophants. She would have grown old anyway, Julie, even if he hadn't written about it."

"But he savored her aging. Every little bit of it in all that careful rhymed artistic anguish."

"What he savored was her beauty. And the tragedy of losing any of it, yes, because he did feel that. But he savored her, as well. Listen a minute. He had more feeling for Andrea than you've ever wanted to admit. You can't blame him if he knew she had started him writing again, and if he was terrified that because of a change in her he might quit."

"Well, he didn't," I said. "He wrote for years. Even after she died. Right up until his death. Pencil in hand to the end."

"He didn't know he would. And anyway, I think he gave her better years, those last ones, than she would have had any other way."

"Oh, I don't know," I said. "How can I be sure? I think it must have made her miserable to have him writing poems about every new wrinkle in her face.

> 'Ill-prepared by those around her
> She slips her moorings for a different sea—
> The ropes of beauty frayed by time.
>   Even the Queens, they say, are being scrapped.'

It's disgusting," I said.

"I didn't know you knew his poems by heart," Jay said.

"And how about the charming one beginning, 'Had we a child whose flesh might us console.'"

"You know he didn't mean that literally," Jay said. "He knew about you."

"It's not that. I don't care about that. But he took it all so seriously, even if he did love her. All right, I agree with what you say, he loved her. But he was so solemn that she lost all sense of humor about herself. He made her brood over her looks as much as he did. She even began using masses of cosmetics, and she never had before. I found a whole cabinet full of them, and we had a fight over it."

"I thought you two never fought."

"An argument really, not a fight. We'd both been sunburned. And she had become so changed."

"Julie, listen. I never knew Andrea well. I never knew her away from Alexander. But I know how great she was for him. God, he was happy. I caught him once just coming out after he had been working. 'You don't know what it's been like,' he said. 'No one knows what it's been like. And now I have her.' And they had fun. You never saw them together so you wouldn't know, but they did. Often when he was with her, he would be looking at her, and he'd just burst out laughing."

"Did he?" I said. "Did he really? Yes, she would have loved that."

"And there was the time they had alone together, often by the ocean."

"Yes, I know about that," I said. "And I understand, I realize, I don't know everything about Andrea. I just loved her so much."

"Yes," he said, "you did."

"And she died so suddenly. Before . . . oh somehow just before anything."

Jay nodded.

"Did you see Alexander when she died?" I asked.

"I met him at the airport," Jay said.

"What did he say?"

"He couldn't talk."

"How do you mean?"

"Just that. He couldn't talk. His jaw was clamped. He could shake his head, but he couldn't say anything."

"I couldn't speak at her funeral," I said. "Not to anyone. But they went ahead and put her in the ground like any other dead thing. No one objected. No one cried out—stop this, stop, it's not possible, it's not right because she was so different. She was so beautiful. I couldn't say it and they just lowered her down and covered her with earth and no one said she was so rare that the ground above where she is buried will be different and the grass there will grow greener than grass grows anywhere."

"Those are Alexander's words," Jay said.

He was right. They were. They were Alexander's words.

"Don't, Julie," Jay said to me. "Don't cry."

"I'm not," I said, and I was gathering her notes and appointment books and the pictures of her on which Alexander had written all into a single pile.

"Here," I said. "You take all these. Perhaps they'll help some biographer writing about him now, or some scholar wanting to know how he worked and the sequence of his words or the reasons for them. You take them, Jay. Only, give them back to me."

And the last words, they should be Alexander's too. He used them to describe and dedicate all his last poems, and I use them the same way for all the words I have tried to say about her:

In Memoriam: Andrea

Tell me, Lord, are these roots dead
Where still the heart sends up new blossoms?
And tell me, Lord, if at their head
A thousand flowers start to grow
From this an aging poet's hands,
Whose is the power that moves him so?
Give time to him who carves the rose
And curls the lips of lilies down,
That barer earth may come to know
This gift, her flowers.

The Thousand Springs

raining.

                                          Sun.

    No church this day due to river flooding. Fields sodden. All the animals affected, but none so skittish as the horses. Unable to comb ("curry," R. would say) them, and can ride only on the few high paths.
    Michael says he has never seen such rains, nor the water so high, and this in 71 years! Which is the more astounding, that he has never seen such a thing, or that anyone could survive so many years in this . . . place?
    Read Poe last night as had resolved to do. Truly an inferior writer. Nothing to compare with H. S. Harrison. His (Poe's) resuscitated fame of the modish, or critical, and transitory sort, of that I am sure.

                                          Tues.

    Birds I have heretofore not seen are found in all our trees and even along the eaves of the outbuildings. Yesterday the sun shone! We rushed blankets and bedding and oh boots boots boots outside to dry. Blessed dryness; blessed absence of the horrid wet. The walls of

The Thousand Springs

our bedroom (2nd storey!) are damp. Kendra has persistent cough, but, D.V., the sun will have restored her. R. spent *entire* day trying to dry milch cows. I baking, ironing, separating milk. Try to think of literature each day. And read each evening: Poe again; and the great, great Harrison.

Secret: I would like to write a story. Not just little sketch this time, but a real story. About the sea. Or ocean. And its long dry white beach. Someday!

Michael sits inside all day. Is in foul humor and will do nothing useful. Says there will be more rain. So sure. How can *he* know? Trying man. Even, yes I will write it—disgusting. Stood shredding the last, so difficultly obtained, newspaper while studying the western sky and using against its neutral face (surely it is neutral, is it not?) the most abusive language. Foul-mouthed abusive old man. My Father once said, "Adjustment to nature is love of God." Wise words. Shall try to observe them. Adjust and accept.

                                                           Wed.

Hardest rains yet! River over all the banks, and crest not yet arrived at County Dip! Men out all night driving, half-swimming stock to McDermott's Ridge. Floor damp under our feet. Water oozing up through cracks. Heretofore I had not known there were cracks in floor.

Day spent baking (flour damp!), cooking, separating milk, ironing clothes dry.

Michael inside by stove ALL day. Says he has the 'flu. Won't bathe. Smells. Disgusting. Andrew brings him sacks of piñon nuts which he roasts and they share by the stove—cracking, spitting, muttering together. Laughing. A. kind, I am glad to say, as I would wish in my son, but is he overly docile? Yet where in this land can/could he wrest any spirit? Any true determination? Any PRIDE? In a house that smells? Must stop. ACCEPT.

I am truly grateful, truly, for my children. Kendra better, thank God. She is not a strong child, but TRIES. Andrew quite different.

Strong as a man, *he* says. Gulps his soup at dinner from his own childhood's handleless mug, won't use another, yet sits by Michael and teases, yes *teases,* him about the weather, and makes all laugh. True. Yet he, A., is no trouble to me, and in truth does the work of a man grown, though he is turned only twelve. In feature he is unlike me, I think, in all but nose. My mind wanders—shameful! Remember: CONCENTRATE. So are ALL things done.

Friday

It rains. Rain standing deep on the ground and it still rains. Rain on rain. Can see no mts. now, just rain. Rain, and rain seen through rain; rain become our windows, and our walls. We all sit, sleep, eat downstairs. No protection against the damp—the lot of us together steaming and close.

Stop. Must concentrate! Day spent baking, drying bedding over stove, separating milk. Continue to read novels of Henry Sydnor Harrison each night. Determined to better my mind and soul under and against all circumstances. Read Bible, too. No more Poe, for A. has removed all the vols., even the poems (Poe's I mean), to his bunk. Wants them for his.

AND, I begin a story. It is to be set, that is the setting of the story is to be, on a vast, dry strip of beach, and the seagulls spinning like motes in the sunlight overhead. I work fifteen min. each night. At the table.

Sat.

All the bedding wet, cannot dry it, and still it rains. Intermittent and drizzling, but rain. R. says the stock suffer in the feet. I am meant to feel concern for them. The truth is, I will write it here—I hate the stock.

I confess to yelling at R. this night. Must not do so again.

Paper I write on here is damp. Wood damp. Sputters and gives off poor heat. We all shiver. What sort of land is this with rain, when it does rain, that wounds, and mountains like hands raised against us.

Must set bread to rise. ACCEPT.

Monday

This morning I opened out the closets and found my last, only velvet gown . . . mildewed. Like a dead child I cradled it in my arms.

I iron clothes dry, bake, iron again. No hope of washing. Neither ourselves nor our clothes. Wood very damp; fires sputter and are slow. I make soup and nurse M., who is better. Kendra sits with him.

River to crest at week's end. R. and A. out constantly raising banks around the stock in the low pastures. I try to prepare warming meals. Make bread pudding. Raisins already plumped out from the damp! Heretofore I have never seen such a thing. Amazing. Seasonings also (Cinnamon and allspice are all I use; I never put nutmeg in my bread pudding) swelled and packed from damp.

Read 15 min. each night. Always my dear Harrison. PERSEVERE.

Monday (Got yesterday's day wrong.)

M. better. Truly, he did have the influenza. Sleeps now; eats soup. Pray rest of us remain well and do not take it. I make strong soup for us all as well, and set bread, separate milk, clean kitchen THOROUGHLY. Good demeanor all day; no reading.

Tuesday

I add to the wet by weeping.

Thursday, Feb. 24

Praise God all my life, my son is restored to me. He had stayed and sheltered two days and the night on the high meadow caring for two of the stock. R. said he never worried, and it is true that he slept (exhaustion?) the entire night through, and when A. came in leading the heifer and calf R. but went out to him, saying no criticism, but helped to rub the animals dry. Now A. sleeps by stove, clothes, mud, and all, and I let him be. Wood sputters with damp, and the light therefore flickers over him. I think he has never been happier than he is in these man-imitating days. I hate this land, God forgive me, but I do. This child-stealing land. How shall they have *time* to grow, such children? Even Kendra, ten, sits up late to rub the horses' feet. None step on her. Her cough is much improved, thank God.

Must build up fire, iron clothes dry.

Tomorrow, I promise self, shall read. Must separate milk, too.

But, praise God, I must, for A.'s return.

Sunday

The river lowers.

There is mud everywhere. On the table legs, the sides of the stove. Everywhere. We all wear boots in the house, to the delight of the children. We all smell. Like the stock. We are disgusting.

I bake, make soup, iron clothes dry. Iron sheets. All of them dirty as we cannot wash, yet I iron them. Iron over mud. Disgusting.

Andrew reads Poe all evening, and holds his calf for its warmth. His calf, now, as R. gave it to him. I clean kitchen and read. Reread the third, great chapter of Harrison's *V V'S EYES*. Surely one of the most beautiful (sustained) passages in all lit. I admit my own feeble efforts fall far short. But, I *keep* trying. The beach I write about, it is to be covered with the palest (whitest? most golden? Exact word important, certainly.) sand, very clean and dry and fine. This, the sandy beach, rises gently to large flat stones, or rocks, and on them a woman walks from the direction of the town. This is but the beginning, of course. There is to be more. I think it is not unpromising.

Monday

Andrew goes camping. CAMPING! R. lets him. He, A., says the mud smells rich. RICH. R. laughs. Says it will indeed make us richer for the land will be better than ever. From the river silt, which is valuable for crops, is what he means.

I wash clothes, table and legs, stove. I bathe. Wood difficult and house cold yet, but I manage. Will NOT be dirty even if must bathe cold. Set bread now, cut bones for soup, find old cloth for teat for calf, and mend.

The night is mine.

That is just a line I wrote here.

Thurs.

Several days' lapse. All as usual. I bake. Read Harrison while bread rises. Joy. Joy. So weepy, however, I am become.

Worked two hours on story. TWO HOURS. Time fled. True. I was not aware of it. Feel story is not without some merit. But the ending . . . that is something of a problem, I admit. Cannot think how to end. PERSEVERE.

Throat scratchy.

Friday

Sunshine. True. Perfectly clear day with sunshine. Blue sky everywhere, clear as clear and the mountains sharp as shells against it. It dazes my eyes. The truth is, my eyes pain me. Even reading hurts. And I am drowsy as well. Fell off to sleep over table last night (night before? no matter) to be awakened by kind touch of A. on my arm. Kind, kind boy. No teasing for all the pages, half-pages, and bits of note-paper with my story on. Kind boy. Such a pity he did not, nor did Kendra, get my eyebrows. Strange. I thought one of them surely would.

CONCENTRATE. Must. Head strange. Confess that this, this writing, these actual lines here I mean, being written in bed. Heretofore I have never done such a thing. R. sent me up early. Said he would prepare noon meal, and clean kitchen. Also separate milk. True. Urged extra sweaters and blanket on me. Tea, too, to come later. Even watched me up the stairs. True. Imagine!

The above are the last fourteen and only known surviving entries, on sixteen and one-third bound quarto pages, comprising in its entirety the final and sole remaining section of the recently discovered, self-titled "Personal Journals" of Bertha Hudson Little, mother of Andrew Little, the writer.

The Valley of Zibelu

The young man came into the Valley from the south, where the cities were and where there were many men of all sorts. He walked because there was no way to ride into the Valley, and he walked slowly because he was unused to walking. So it was only after a long time that he came to the big hut which stood in the front, a little separate from the five other ones. The old man, his uncle, was sitting on the ground before the hut, waiting, for they had been expecting him, and they had known as soon as he had come over the hills into the Valley. He stopped in front of the old man, and feeling very solemn because of the occasion and because of his Anglican priest's clothes with the hat and shoes, which they had not seen on him before, ever, he saluted his uncle gravely, in the formal native fashion.

"Greetings, my father."

"Greetings, son of my elder brother."

"Greetings," said the young man again. Then he took a large white linen handkerchief out of his pocket and wiped the sweat from his neck and face.

"Ntia," the old man called, "bring the stool."

Immediately, as if she had been waiting, a small old woman popped out of the door of the hut. She was carrying a European folding stool. Somehow they had got hold of it, and kept it, suspecting that since nothing remained the same anymore, they might one day have use for such a thing. She placed it on the ground to the right of the old man, and taking one quick, shy glance at the young man and the strange black clothes, she went back inside the hut.

The young priest sat down gratefully on the stool, glad to have it for he would have had to stand otherwise. He would not have been willing to sit with the old man in the dust. Not in these clothes. He was glad, too, that the old woman had gone back inside the hut and had not stayed on to stare at him, as he had seen the women do with Europeans—stare blankly, openly, never thinking anything so unlike themselves would notice, much less mind.

He looked down at his uncle. "I came as soon as I could," he said to the old man. "As soon as I heard."

The old man looked up at him and had to squint his eyes against the afternoon sun that slanted across the young man's shoulders.

"It took time to get permission from the Bishop, from my chief," the young man said. "I had to get permission to leave, to come here. Even for a man to go when his father dies he must ask to go. It is very strict, very very strict for us. There is hard . . . there is much rule for us, there. But as soon as I got permission, then I came."

Still the old man did not answer.

"I came as soon as I could," the young man said again.

The old man said softly, "It has been a long time. Even before now it was a long time. Even your father before he died expected you. We have expected you for a long time but you did not come until now."

"Yes, yes, I know. And my mother?"

"She is in Nlosheni, with her brother's son. There is corn there. There is no corn here," he said, and made a little circle with his hand at the burnt land around them. "She has gone where there is corn."

"Yes," the young man said.

He looked down at the dust on his shoes and on the bottoms of his trousers. With his handkerchief he brushed off his shoes, and he dusted and creased his trousers carefully. Then he took his handkerchief and dusted and polished and polished again the heavy cross hanging around his neck. Basically the cross was bronze, but on it, in a low bas relief, was the figure of Christ outlined in gold plate. It was the cross of his ordination, given to him by the Bishop. The old man watched him cleaning it, watched him openly and blankly and thoroughly as he polished and cleaned the cross and ran his fingers

The Valley of Zibelu

over the slick, smooth metal. He even dusted the cord by which it hung and then tucked the end of the cross back into his vest.

He looked about him at the lifeless huts. All made of old, drying straw and reeds, and how precariously, it seemed to him now, they perched on the dust. For that is all the ground was, dust, layers and layers of dust, except for a place here and there where it had cracked open and showed through the wound the hard dry dirt beneath. They never try to irrigate here, the young man thought. They never try to improve. They are helpless, helpless, and they blame everyone else. He rubbed his face and head with the handkerchief again and turned to the old man.

"Is there no one here at all then?" he said. "No cattle? Does no one farm your lands now?"

The old man looked startled. "But you know," he said, "that we do not live all together on top of each other like the ants or the Soto." Everyone, surely, knew this, but who could know what the young man had forgotten in the City. "Here," said the old man, "here, as is right, each man has his own kraal and his own lands and lives in them with those who are his people."

"No no, I know that," the young man said. "Surely. But here and in the other kraals where I came, all through the Valley, there is no one. I saw no one but a few women. Why don't they do something for the land? Are they gone? Are they too lazy even?"

"No, oh no," said the old man gently. "They are here," and he pointed vaguely around. "They were perhaps looking for a cow that had strayed, when you came by. Or an ox even. Or they have perhaps gone away to see a friend for a while. And you know, there is no corn."

"My brother will help them. He will be a good chief," the young man said. "He will be better than any before. Better than I would have been."

To this the old man said nothing, but he no longer stared at his nephew. He made instead a little pile of dust with one hand and smoothed it out with the other.

"You know that," the priest insisted. "My brother will be a good chief. My own father even loved him best. He will be a fine chief. Everything will be better here now."

"Yes," said the old man, out of politeness, "and perhaps there will be rain, surely."

"My brother will not be as my father was. My brother will bring water in long ditches. And he will bring machines to help plant, and food for the ground so what is planted will grow. He knows about these things. And he knows about these things because of the church school, because of what the good priests taught him. You will see, everything will be different. Everything."

The old man nodded in mildest agreement. He was not one to argue with a chief, even one who ran away to the City. Who could tell when a chief might change his mind and demand his rights.

"But everyone must help," the priest was saying, "and they cannot go away all the time to make visits and they can't do nothing all the time."

"They are working," the old man said earnestly, "they are working. It is only for a little while they have gone away. Perhaps to rest for a little. Or to find a cow. Just for a little."

He nodded seriously at his own words, and he looked politely down, but then began studying his nephew's shoes, and his trousers, and then raised his eyes and stared at the heavy bronze-and-gold cross. At once the young man put his hand over the cross, to protect it, and when his uncle lowered his head he felt ashamed.

"And you, are you well, my father?" he asked softly.

"Yes, we eat meat," the old man said formally. And then, "But you are hot. We will drink now." He called to his wife, then turning to his nephew he said, "There is only milk. We have no corn for beer."

The old woman came out immediately, again as if she had been waiting just inside the door. She carried a jug of amazi, the heavily soured milk they drank. She came bowed down, as to an honored stranger, one much older and more respected than herself, as to a chief, perhaps. She handed him the jug, and he, wanting to help her, turned quickly to take it. But she was not expecting the move, and bumped into him, and for a second the jug jostled between their four hands, and then fell, spewing the thick white stuff out over the young man's pants and shoes, and onto the ground. He leaped up

The Valley of Zibelu

and screamed at the old woman and cursed her violently, and she fled back inside the hut. The old man sat quietly the whole time; he moved not at all except to inch his knee out of the path of the slowly spreading milk, but he said nothing.

With no one to yell at, the young man stood for an instant bereft, then grabbed up the camp stool and put it down away from the pool of soured milk. He sat down and began to wipe his pants and shoes. He even dusted his hat, and then put it back on the ground. He saw that at least the jug was not broken, and he reached over and set it upright for it still had in it some of the soured milk. The feel of the jug, of the thick clay pottery, reminded him of how, when he was a child, he would hug the jug to his chest, cherish it, before taking his share of the milk. Food and drink both it had been, and comforting. This very aunt had brought him amazi when his father had dragged him home from the missionaries' school, the first time he had run away, and he had lain in his mother's hut, crying and frightened. His aunt had crept in bringing him the drink in a little dark jug. Yes, and she had stayed beside him until he had finished it all, and she had sung little riddles to him, cradling him almost, like a baby almost, until he had gone to sleep. Now watching the old man sprinkle dust over the thin trickles of the drink, which he knew was preciously rare in this, the dry season, he felt a jerking, painful anger.

"She is getting old. And clumsy," he said harshly.

"Yes," said the old man politely.

"Where is my father buried?" he asked.

"On the hill."

There was no need to say which hill. All the chiefs were buried on the big hill not far from his uncle's hut, except for the few chiefs of great fame or strength or power who had been taken on a longer voyage to the great mountain, at the far end of the Valley, overlooking most of the lands where they had ruled, or thought they ruled. His father, then, had not been that great a chief. Well, he had known it.

"I will go there now," the priest said, rising.

"I will go with you," the old man said.

"No, no. It is a long way for you. I will go alone. I know the way. I want to go alone, just myself."

"Yes," said the old man. "Yes, surely." But he got up, and still saying "yes, yes surely," he followed his nephew on the path that rose to the big hill.

It was a steep climb, but the old man did not seem to mind it. Gradually he took over the lead and went up at a steady, unrelaxing pace, only waiting now and then, with a little smile, for his nephew, who was tired and unused to climbing and most of all hampered by having to walk carefully in his leather shoes.

When they came to the top, the old man stepped back and let the other go ahead. There were many graves, but the new one was the first one, the one nearest the edge of the hill. The young man walked to it and his uncle came quietly behind him.

"Where is the guard?" he asked the old man.

"He was here at first. I think now he has gone to find a cow which was lost two weeks ago. Or maybe it was an ox even. His son could not go to find it because his son is in the mines."

The young man nodded and turned back to the grave. He held his hat stiffly behind him and stood before the flat covering of stones. He knew the old man was watching him.

"Are you not going to make prayers?" the old man asked. And although his wrinkled face was bland, there was no lowering of his gaze to deny the amusement in his voice.

Self-consciously the young man set his hat on a rock and slowly knelt down. He clasped his hands before him, but he could think of nothing. No flow of words. Not in English, nor his own language. He reached into his inner pocket and brought out his little prayer book and holding it before him began to read, more or less at random, whatever he came across that would seem to serve. He read the general confession, the collect for communion, and one of the psalms. But at the end of the first verse he stopped. He remained kneeling, staring above the book at the dry stones in front of him. It was several seconds before he realized that he had stopped. He crossed himself and started to rise, but then, in a stately manner, made a large, slow cross in the air above the grave.

He dropped his hand and glanced at the old man, who was grinning openly, his shoulders shaking a little.

The Valley of Zibelu

"You fool," the young man said in English. "You fool. You savage. You bloody savage."

And the old man nodded and grinned at him, more and more amused by the increased volume of the words.

The young man turned away and tucked his prayer book back in his coat pocket. He was ready to go, but he could not say so to the old man.

"There should be a marker, a stone," he said, instead.

The old man shrugged indifferently.

"I want something special for my father," the young man said.

"Oh, yes," the old man said, "yes." And waited.

With irritation the young man took off his coat, dropped it on a large boulder, and began moving and rolling the stones from the head of the grave into a pile. The stones were all shapes and sizes and uneven, and they kept rolling back off the pile or monument and he often had to put the same stone back again and wedge it into place before he could start on another one. The old man squatted on the ground while he worked and watched with interest, nodding approval from time to time.

The sweat began to run into his eyes, and he worked more slowly but with more patience, taking more care with each additional stone, and he felt sorry when it was finished, when he was done.

"See, it's a cross," he said to the old man.

"A cross?" the old man said, and came to stand beside him, and together they looked at the stone pile that was meant to be a cross laid flat upon the ground.

"A big cross," the young man said, "like this one," and he pointed to his own bronze-and-gold one hanging around his neck.

The old man looked at it and then back at the clump of rocks. "A cross," he said. "Yes, surely, that is what it is, a cross." And he looked at his nephew with a wide grin and nodded cheerfully. "Oh certainly," he said, "a cross. Surely, a cross."

"Savage. Native," the young man said in English, and the old man nodded and grinned at him.

"Fool," the young man said, but he grabbed at the cord around his neck and tugged at it, having to do so twice before it broke, and pulled the cross from his vest, the cord trailing free from his neck, and then he knelt and placed the cross at the base of his pile of stones. He made a little place for it, between two stones, and set it in carefully and wedged it there so it would be protected. When he finished he looked over at his uncle, but the old man was standing politely away from him and with his head turned, not looking now, and the young man sat down and rested among the stones.

He thought now for a few moments of his father and of the nature of the hardness of his father's life. He began to pray, not taking out his prayer book, but reciting the prayers from memory and in English. He would recite all the proper prayers he knew and all in English, making use of the excellent memory that had got him through school and seminary, and when he made a mistake he would go back and start again at the beginning until he had said each one through perfectly. The Twenty-third Psalm and the Lord's Prayer, and the opening prayers for the Burial of the Dead, and even the long Ninetieth Psalm, which comes in the service for burial, and which he stumbled over again and again and started again and again, going on in the doubly unfamiliar old English words, "Lord, thou hast been our refuge, from one generation to another . . ." until finally he had said it all the way through without mistake. Now he was finished. He picked up his hat from off the rock where he had placed it, and his coat, and he put them on, and then, not bothering to look at his uncle, he started back into the Valley. The old man followed silently all the way and let him pick his own way down.

When they reached the hut, the young man did not sit down. He was sore from unaccustomed walking and he was tired, but he had resolved not to spend the night here. He would start at once on the return journey to the railroad junction, and back to the City and his Church.

"I will come again, my father," he said when he had explained that he could not stay.

"Yes," said the old man, but he knew it was not so.

"I will send you money."

"That will be good. The land is very dry."

"You should irrigate, bring water. The land could flourish."

"Yes."

The old woman did not come out of the hut, so the young man said his formal farewells only to his uncle, and then he started on the path that went out of the Valley to the south, where the cities were.

The Valley of Zibelu

As soon as he had gone, the old woman came out of the hut. The old man asked her for his blanket, for the evenings were apt to be cool, and she brought it to him and placed it carefully on his shoulders. He told her it was too bad about the amazi being knocked over by the clumsy boy, because the cows did not give much milk in the dry season. She said she would go to the spring to get water instead, and maybe tomorrow or the next day the cow would give milk again.

He said yes, maybe that was so.

Then he rose and started back up the big hill. It took him much longer to climb this time, but even so he reached the top before dark. He took off his blanket and began the work of taking down the stones that his nephew had piled up. He went at it casually but steadily, rolling them aside in any direction. Two he rolled off the hill itself to watch them bounce their way toward the Valley . . . clumpf, clumpf, clumpf . . . all the way down. It did not take him long. He pulled the cross out from between the two rocks which had been at the base of the pile, and he moved those rocks away too. He told his ancestors over the grave that if he had had a goat he would have killed it, but he did not have one because of the dry season and there being no corn. He pledged them the next goat that he got, if he got one.

He took the cross and tied the broken cord together and hung it around his neck. But it was heavy there, and the cord cut into the bare skin at the back of his neck, so he took it off and slung it instead over his shoulder and across his chest with the cross dangling under his arm. He put his blanket over his other shoulder, then he started back down the hill. He hoped very much that his wife had been able to find some wild spinach to eat, or some roots, for he was hungry after all his climbing. Anyway, if not, he might get something from his father's sister's daughter, just across the Valley from him. And they would be sure to get meat tomorrow he thought happily, when he went to visit his elder brother's son, he who was now Chief of all the Valley.

The Rock Garden

It was necessary to say that millions died in the concentration camps in Germany. And millions before that in the Belgian Congo. Or in slave ships on the Atlantic. Children terrified and adults worked to death. Mothers frantic, holding too thin babies. Firm-bodied young men with terror in their faces. She could have been one of them, could be one of them now in Vietnam, dying any day, every day. This day. It was necessary to remember, never to forget.

So she spoke to herself each morning as she woke in the midst of the luck of her life, aware of its preciousness. Sixty-eight and with a husband living. Well-off to rich, depending on the viewer's finances. Traveled. Healthy. Even having aged well, staying slim, handsome, with the clearest round blue eyes of the sort that never fade.

"We have been considering Australia again for the next trip." Her voice. "Doing it more thoroughly, to see the rare birds. We have been so interested in birds."

How do the rich pay their debts? she wondered. All this luck, this money, this health. This free, and freeing, time so there could be the music and birds, the travel, the beautiful presents. Courtesy. Great courtesy. ("You were so extremely kind when we were there last summer we did want to send you this little remembrance of our good times together. We had such fun selecting it.") Constant courtesy.

He was retired. Was cleverer than she, but less humane. Was vain, hurt by age, stranded in some limbo between solitude and

The Rock Garden

company, some battlefield of loss where the half-deaf go. He tried, retried, bought, repaired hearing aids. "It has the most minute battery invented," he said. "Transistorized. No, no, you have to look much more carefully than that. Try. There are three of them, see? No, you haven't looked really close. Now try again."

"If we were meant to fly, the Lord would have given us wings, my mother used to say. Oh, she *was* old-fashioned. She taught me how to do this," braiding flowers for a teenaged granddaughter and her young friend, "and how to blow on a blade of grass to make it hoot. She showed us both, me and my brother. Dear Tag." He had been killed in the war, World War I, that was. Her greatest, only, grief, that bitter death. "My mother preferred him, and I am glad she did, you see, because he had so little time." Meant what she said, too, braiding flowers into a colored stream, eyes blue under her bright straw hat. So human, so courteous. So good, remembering in the morning the tortured dead, blue eyes to the familiar ceiling, trying not to be only rich and lucky, but rich and lucky and good.

"Don't you think we owe them remembering?" she had asked him.

"It can't matter to them," he said. Logic.

"But it does matter. At least, it matters to me."

In September they traveled all the way to south Texas to see the whooping cranes. She rose at four and touched his shoulder (he could not hear the alarm) and they went out in the wet predawn on land flat as a mirage and watched the sun bring the birds up, watched the birds run out of the reeds with a machine's clumsiness, the flap and stretch of wings pounding the cold air for support and then, as slowly as if the air were a stairway, rising up, forward, up, and gone.

Later, in Florida, they saw the flamingoes. And the threatened alligators. They saw and appreciated all the endangered species.

"We *should* see them since we are among those fortunate enough to be able to do so, and it is such an opportunity. We feel we ought to," she said.

The species did not know they were dying. They had that gift, were dying unawares. She longed for that, to die sleeping, in bed, unknowing and unafraid. For wasn't that the worst, she thought, knowing? To see the horror coming day by day, closer and closer, to know it and not be able to help. She read that the camp inmates knew, denied in their minds they knew, did know, admitted, wept, cried, begged, and still were tortured, still died, all the same. There had been those just like herself. She had read about them—Bruno Bettelheim's family, dying in concentration camps. They who had been lucky all their lives until their ends. Which did not mean it had to happen to her. It did not do, she understood that, to be morbid. But could not stop trying to imagine the unimaginable, could not understand the luck of her life, could make no sense, and no use, of having been one to survive.

"Alan and I found each other before I knew he might inherit money," she had said, a burst, outburst, of confidence made beside a crystal lake. Quite true. All the good that had come to her had been uncalculated and unearned. "We never worked for this money, we both know that." But kept it, spent it, nonetheless.

"The lions were so wonderfully arrogant." Talking to a friend's listening children. "And terribly healthy, but so arrogant. Thank heavens, they had *no* ticks. A scientist friend told me they would be covered with ticks, and I had dreaded that, but these were so clean. Our driver, such a funny man, insisted on going right off the road and into the brush. My poor spine, pancaked . . . but I have been doing exercises, just the way you children are supposed to, and am so much better."

The lion account was from Africa. Their second trip, to do it better. Avoiding the Union of South Africa, for reasons of conscience. Sorry for the poverty. Overtipping. But loving the animals. Rolls of film taken of the animals and none of the people.

She had been afraid in Africa. Afraid of the poverty. Afraid of the blacks. Afraid she would not recognize the ones she knew as their features melted in the blackness of their skin. "Look at the springboks leap up for no reason," she had said. "Why do they do that?" The guide answered in his tongue, and all the natives laughed.

She had turned her face, eyes straight ahead, one arm pointing determinedly at the animals, her face smiling. She knew sex in a laugh when she heard it. Yet it was the same guide who sat half-hour after half-hour beside her, begging for please one more bracelet made from the brilliant flowers he brought her and loved to wear on his beautiful black background of skin. And she, showing him her ways, told herself that not even in her secret heart must she think she was improving him, for surely she was learning from him, too.

"But the little koalas in Australia," she went on, and the children came closer, "they were my favorites. They put up their paws like this," doing it herself, herself a cunning little blue-eyed koala, so willing to be funny, such a good sport and companion, so charming with little children who did not breathe in order to watch her better, "just like this they do it, and rub rub rub their noses. Rub rub rub. They are enchanting little creatures, and not extinct at all. But it is a very smug country," turning to the adults for this, "and so very comfortable. We rather did *not* care for that."

She thought. She thought behind her smiles, her courtesy, her concert-going, behind her carefully chosen gifts and cards of thanks or condolence, her notes at Christmas (always nondenominational, always UNICEF to help poor children). She thought with helpless honesty that she had no special courage or strength, that she hated pain and feared fear, that she was not worth her long life's many gifts, and still with all this allowed her, still she wanted peace, health, her end to come some long space of time away and in her sleep and she unknowing and unafraid. She thought, calling herself foolish, that the only anguish in her life was that she had no anguish, and no reason for that sparing.

She kept on being delightful for her own grandchildren and her friends' grandchildren; cheerful for her sons and her daughter, her son-in-law, her daughters-in-law. She remained the best of friends for her troubled friends ("How it would please us if you would join us this Thanksgiving and make it so much warmer for us both...."), consistently generous to poor musicians, consistently charming to all. "The little koalas put up their paws, just like this, and rub rub rub. . . ."

She read the digest of the Nuremberg Trials by Lord Russell of Liverpool, the British prosecutor. Read all the details, looked at all the pictures. Resisted the pressure to read further volume after volume about it. "Don't you think," she said, "that to read so much in such detail about it is, I don't like to use the word but I will, voyeurism?"

Yet the stories of horror came at her, puncturing the floor of her consciousness in the same way she had seen anti-aircraft flak, in films, come up at the photographing airplane and burst through its floor of safety in strange and dangerous flowers. They were unavoidable, the stories of people suffering, straining uselessly, knowing. One, just a photograph, from Vietnam, of a man running, his mouth clothes-hanger shape with fear and strain, running, a child in his arms (the child dead, blood seeping from its ear, quite dead, but he did not know and how could she tell him?), running across a rice field, mud on his thin muscled thigh, one foot raised forever. His wife behind him running also, a child shielded against her breast, a younger child, living perhaps. Both adults terrified, running, and nothing stopping it, one foot always raised. She saw it when she did not sleep, saw it with no need to look at the picture she had cut out and slipped between the programs from the winter's concerts. Visiting her son, she saw it in the dark in the slightly unfamiliar room, the others in the house near her and all sleeping, and in her mind that frozen running, the distorted mouth, the soft rice plants, the child, the foot raised, the terror, the child, and nothing ever helping.

"Would you let us," she wrote, "take the family's youngest Alan to the coast this summer? He has never seen it, and the birds are a marvel there. And more, we have not yet had the pleasure of taking him on a special trip, all alone, with us, and we would love to do so."

She and the child collected shells. "That one's too small to hear the sea in," the boy said to her. "You need a conch for that. Or any old thing that's big and hollow. A jug."

The Rock Garden

"But I like the small ones because they are so sweet," she said.

"I like them because they are easy to find," he said. They laughed; his teeth were like the crests of tiny waves. A darling, darling boy. She was so lucky.

They had their own cabin, their beach, their own ocean, it seemed, its roar filling up the air. Deaf, did he hear the ocean in his own ear's whorls? She had taken to asking silly questions in the sleepless dark. Got up instead. Read. And when the grandson rose, went swimming with him in the warm dawn. In her psychedelic suit and flowered cap, dipping in on her long crane's legs, careful, enjoying, sensible. She thought (oh, I am a silly woman, I surely am) the salt water on her cheeks might be the tears she had not needed to weep.

Sitting on the beach chairs beside the cabin, the boy at their feet on the ground, watching the water burn at sunset, she jumped as her husband touched his hand slowly to the side of his neck and brought it away with blood. It's starting, she thought. But he was studying on his palm a mosquito crushed in his usual careful way, and was commenting to the boy on the blood transfused from his body and now spread on his hand. Then he leaned to the side and wiped his hand clean on the thin grass coming up through the sand.

They returned home, northward, at the end of summer. "Oh, we could never give up the season's concerts," she said in answer, "and we are used to the cold, when it comes."

They decided to make a rock garden. He made the design, taking days to perfect it. They would do it all themselves. He would search for rocks, from their acres or those of friends, or even sometimes buy them. He would drive out in the car going at slow speeds, the car no sound to him, his eyes going back and forth from the highway to the countryside for forms or colors of rocks that he wanted. She did the carrying and placing. She learned how she could squat and rise straight up, a rock cradled in her arms. She found she could carry heavier stones than he. Nothing daunted her.

"Aren't we lucky," she said, "that we didn't do it before?"

And she learned to lever and how to roll rocks down planks, always shielding him from the fact that she managed the heaviest ones. She would kneel and roll the big round ones, tumbling them end over end to the approved position. But best of all she liked the middle-sized rocks she could carry in her arms, the ones which on warm days (for she had given up work gloves) she would stand holding with their sunbaked surface against her bare arms and hands. Her unshed tears, she called them, shaking her head at her silliness, her unshed tears she had been spared.

She learned to make borders. Learned to shape unexpected designs from the combinations of different shapes. Learned how to brace against the slope and how to save her toes from being crushed. "I must have New England in my blood," she said. "I sleep so well."

In fall, in the cooler weather, he tired of it. She hesitated to show disagreement, lest it seem her strength was outlasting his and he be wounded. So she sat, her long spine curved over a book, reading beside him on the glassed-in porch. But when he was absorbed inside the house, she returned to the garden and her rocks. She arched over them to find just the one she wanted next, her eyes alert for the right size and color, for the little stones she would need for bracing, the big ones she would have to lift slowly and carry in her arms to their new homes. She loved to stand above the empty space when she had raised a rock, holding it close, her breath coming well earned and cold into her working lungs.

She feared the winter. Feared the bad weather, but when it came the rocks did not freeze and split, only became coated with ice and snow, though over and over again she would go out and sweep them clear with a soft broom and see their shapes again.

"You've forgotten to feed the birds," he said.

"Oh, shame on me," she said. "Aren't I silly? I've gone over entirely to stone." She cut lard in pea-sized pieces, crumbed bread, and cast both for the whirlpool of birds descending.

"Charming," she said. But her smile moved her lips only. "Charming. Birdie, birdie."

"Why," she asked him, "with the resurgence of German literature, is there no book on the triumph over France, or a journal of the life of a concentration camp guard?"

He had not heard. Like a reading lamp, his concentration was turned only in the direction he faced. She moved within his line of sight so he could see she spoke.

"There's all this talk of a new German literature," she said firmly. "It's all about Germany's defeat. Why not the joys of an SS guard, or the victory march into Paris?"

His intelligence was sharpened on her. She had caught his interest; he was not being polite.

"An excellent question. As a rule our time favors the criminal over the victim. Capote's book, for example. So in all logic we should focus on the SS. Someday, yes, I envisage an entire literature on this untouched subject. Memoirs of an SS guard's youth. Pseudo-fiction, of course, in the best modern. Then pornography—Sex outside the Gas Chambers."

She said, "There was one job, a guard searched the clothing women had to hang on pegs outside the gas chamber because sometimes mothers tried to hide their children in the clothes."

"Presumably the world of serious literature is not ready for that as art yet. The fall of the Wehrmacht, that's what's selling now."

"I wonder about them."

"Who?"

"The guards who searched the clothes for children."

When it was very cold the snow hardened. Across the tops of the rocks and the sides facing west the snow melted in the daytime and froze again at night until layer after layer sheeted over the rocks. The fresh snow fell on ice then, and thickened, and was pressed down itself by icy rain, which formed a light crystal glaze at first, but froze hard later, at night, or on colder days, covering all the rocks so there was no longer any way to see their shapes. She would walk out, carefully, on crane's legs, and bend over them, searching for her favorites. They no longer had a separate color but were a single mass of the bleached gray, mud-textured white of winter. She curved over them, looking closer. The cold blazed her ears and face, but she would not leave them. She crouched down, shivering and shivering, and pressed her ungloved hands against them, holding the outlines of some as best she could under the thickness of snow.

"Oh my darlings," she said to them. "My darlings."

"What are you doing?" His voice. The essence of him coming down to her. "You've got no coat."

He pulled her up. His hands were warm manacles circling through her cold-stiffened blouse (long sleeves always to cover age's shrinking flesh). He was leading her back to the house, up the steps to their back door, into the kitchen where bands of stainless steel and birch shot out around them.

"Are you unwell?" he demanded of her.

"No," she said, "no." She tore out of his hands. "I'm perfectly well, God forgive me," and she smashed with her fists into the cabinets level with her face once, twice, three times, saying, "I'm perfectly, perfectly well."

The sound was shattering in the room, and she saw him gape, saw a mask fall from him and under it an unfamiliar, startled, alarmed old man.

"So clumsy of me," she said. And let herself lean forward against him, her hands supporting him while seeming to support herself. "So clumsy. Do excuse. The cold must have. . . . Aren't I silly?"

He was too polite to question, or to fuss hard. Just led her, quite unnecessarily but she let him because she wanted to, into the living room and had her lie stretched full length on the couch beside the fire. He set an extra log in the flames, and the warmth melted into her where she lay with her head resting back on a soft pillow and the white and heavily beamed ceiling overhead. They were old beams, carefully chosen and unusually thick, and the adz marks into them made soft shallows softened further by the firelight's shadows. They ran in great parallel rows above her body, and she saw in them the freight cars she had read about last summer. She had been flipping through the pages of the book review section of a Sunday paper, glancing, flipping, and the paragraph leaped off the page and burst into her mind. The siege of Stalingrad. Freight cars outside, filled, packed, with Russian prisoners, then abandoned (how long? forever?), left completely, left on a siding and in the bright sunlight feces and urine dripping down through the cars' wide boards onto the railroad tracks beneath.

The Rock Garden

He was stirring the fire steady for her, caging it. He brought a red wool blanket they had bought in Norway and placed it the wrong, heavy way across her knees. He left to heat soup for lunch, but returned unexpectedly to throw a handful of sea salts into the misshapen mouth of the fire. The ceiling became vibrant with colors, and the room was streaked with the sounds and smells of the salts burning. She turned her face toward the fire.

"Charming," she said. "Charming. Aren't we lucky, that we have them?"

The Judge

The Mexican's name was Baille. "Pronounced 'Buy-ye,'" the Judge liked to explain with amusement, and for the past three months now, at least once every week, the Judge had driven out through the flat countryside to where the Mexican lived to try and make him sign some papers. So far the Mexican would not do it.

"*You'd think I was trying to sell him snake oil,*" the Judge said. "*The old charlatan. I can't help liking him. Last time he came out with the statement that he didn't even have any rights in the claim at all. Just after I had shown him, with genealogical charts, how I had traced him. He says he's Basque, but that's nonsense. The name is pure Spanish. You find it all over this part of the state and in northern Mexico, going back, with a few orthographic variations, for two hundred years. There were never any Basques around here.*"

The Judge would know. He knew about languages and races and the origins of people and their names. He had made a study of such things. He could speak five languages and read two more. He knew Baille personally, too, though it was only in the last year that he had come to know the Mexican well.

"*It's not that he's an important claimant,*" the Judge said. "*His portion is one of the smaller ones. But when it is a question of the heirs in a petition against the States, then it looks better to have all the heirs file. He's the only one who won't sign. One hundred and twenty-seven depositions I've got, two of them from as far away as the state of Oaxaca, and a brief that is easily the most complicated ever submitted in this jurisdiction, and I'm held up by a country school janitor. It's good I can appreciate the humor of it. Nonetheless, time is getting short. I must try to move him along this Sunday. I'll tell you one thing, if I have to drive out to that place of his many more times, I'm going to get the county to do something about that road."*

Not the highway. The Judge did not mean that. The highway was fine; laid flat and dead straight on the ground, it fell before him across the countryside like a clap of thunder, splitting the gray brush in two. On Sunday afternoons it was usually empty, and the Judge's solitary car hummed along at the fifty miles an hour advised by the instruction book as best for breaking in a new car. They had offered to let him keep a state car when he resigned. "No, no," the Judge had said, "you know me better than that."

The first turn off the highway to Baille's came just beyond the railroad crossing. From there the Judge's car followed a gravel road past the country school where the Mexican was janitor. Beyond that there was a bend crowded by willow trees and then a sharp right turn onto a narrow dirt road. Dust spilled out under the wheels and rose up beside the car like a giant gray dog and ran around the curves with it, brushing against the bushes in the narrow places. When the Judge stopped at last before the Mexican's house, dust poured up and over and through the car and on ahead down the road before collapsing back down into the ground again.

The Judge spat out the window to clear his mouth and honked the horn once, then again. Nothing happened. He knew Baille would not come out. He honked again, longer.

"Baille," the Judge yelled out the car window. "Hey, Baille."

"You know, I took a Sears catalog out there to him once. And a big black pencil in case he didn't have one. I told him to put a check by all the things in the catalog he wanted, just go ahead and mark everything he would like to have, anything and everything, and to

keep on marking, and I would tell him to stop when he had used up the money I could make for him in one single year. He wouldn't do it. He wouldn't even look at the catalog. Wouldn't even open it."

The Judge sat in the car staring at the shack and rubbing his nose, which he did in a very distinctive way. He held his hand still and moved his head gently up and down, sliding his nose between his thumb and forefinger. It was occurring to the Judge that it would all be a great deal easier if the Mexican had more of the world's goods, for then there would be more places where pressure could be applied.

The Judge honked again, and called "Baille" louder, but without really expecting any result. He got out of the car and started over to the gate. A short man, with most of his height from the waist up, the Judge walked with his back rigid and his big powerful stomach firmly leading so that he looked in profile like a chair being pushed steadily forward.

Around his feet two bulbs of dust spouted onto his shoelaces and his trouser legs and then settled back down on the tops and sides of his shoes when he stopped before the fence. It was a fence made of barbed wire and mesquite. The wire was a dull color, with rust exploding around the base of each barb, and the untrimmed mesquite posts were knobbed and twisted and so dried up that the old shallow, hand-dug postholes gaped open around them.

The Judge established himself by the main gate post to wait. He lifted a foot to rest it comfortably on one of the lower strands, but the wire twanged loose onto the ground, throwing the Judge forward.

"Damn," the Judge swore. And yelled "Baille!"

"It's true that it is not precisely flattering to be kept cooling my heels outside his fence until it suits him to come out. I need my old bailiff to hail him for me. Still, they have a sense of dignity and pride, these Mexicans. It denies our tempo of doing things. They insist on time, they respect it. And let me make one other point: he has some strange, absolutely perfect sense of just when it is the right time to come out."

The Judge pressed his stomach against the gate, moving it back on the tripled loops of wire that served as hinges. His hand eased along toward the latch. From around a corner of the shack the Mexican ap-

The Judge

peared, walking quickly with little low steps that moved him over the bare ground with no up-and-down movement at all but simply a fast unbroken propulsion forward as steadily efficient as the towing along of rakes or harrows after tractors, or the dragging of dead things behind the low rear bumpers of cars.

He was a man in his fifties, and so short he was forced to tip his head back to look up at the Judge. When he did, the Mexican showed his face with all the flattest angles exposed, showed his quick blinking eyes and soft squashed nose.

"How can you stand the heat out here?" the Judge said in a friendly tone.

The Mexican stared at him with the wild surprise the Judge's lisping Castilian always brought to him, for how was it this man could go on sounding like a drunken bird every time he spoke?

"Doesn't it bother you?" the Judge said again.

"You don't like the heat?" the Mexican said finally, hopefully.

"I can take the heat. It's the dust I really don't like. I swear, if you don't start acting sensibly, Baille, I'm going to get this road blacktopped."

The Mexican peered in amazement at the thin dirt road running along his fence and beneath the Judge's car, for the Judge had just announced that he intended to take an oath to do away with the road in darkness with a coating of perpetual obscurity.

"You don't like the dust then?" the Mexican said, trying again. "There is certainly much dust here. Much dust. You should stay in town. You stay in town, and I will come to visit you there."

"There is an innocence, or rather an obviousness that reminds one of innocence, in some of his ploys. At times it is terribly poignant. A touch . . . not of childishness, they are not childish, these people, he's a grown and very tough man, but a touch of the basic, unconcealed, open human being that can be very moving. Would any of you believe that I feel I have actually learned from him?"

"I think not," the Judge said to the Mexican. "I think not. You might forget to come. But I never forget, do I?" And the Judge began to fan himself slowly, swinging his hat in wide arcs. His clothing was sweated through. "Listen," the Judge said, "why won't you trust me? All I want is to make some money for you. Why won't you do what I tell you?"

"Don't think the irony of it has escaped me. Mrs. Easterbury reminded me only the other night that I was the one who got him his job. Otherwise he might not even be around here. Well, I don't regret it. He came to me for help about two years ago. I'd hardly spoken to him before, but he knew who I was, so of course I had to help him. His wife had just left him, and he had some scheme in mind, some absurd plan for getting her back. I got him the job as janitor. I told the school board he would never steal. I took the responsibility for that and gave them my assurance, and he never has stolen a thing."

"No papers," the Mexican said, shaking his head. "No papers for signing. Absolutely no."

"You can sign your name," the Judge said. "I've seen it written down at the courthouse."

The Mexican neither moved nor spoke, but the Judge became instantly alert, for he knew, just as he would have in a courtroom, that the Mexican was running inside, running and running while he was standing still. The Judge was sure of it.

"What's the matter with your name on the records?" the Judge said. "Hm? What's wrong with it?"

"Nothing, nothing," the Mexican said. "It's my mother's name for me, why not? So if you don't like it, what will you do? Shoot me?" And he burst into a fit of giggles snuffled out against the back of his hand. For the phrase in Spanish was *Fuegame,* and it could mean either "fire me," as from a job, or "shoot me," as with a gun. Months ago when the Mexican had first said it, the Judge had been so delighted he had laughed out loud, and after a few seconds of uncertainty, Baille had joined in, laughing harder and harder.

"Their humor. Even when used as the most pathetically obvious smoke screen, still it is always appealing. Superb, poised, and proud. It's dour and simple, yet with sophistication, too, and with that special cast of appreciating language. That's what I relish most of all, the gift of language that they have. You see it right from the earliest days of the nation's history and down through all the major shifts in the language itself. They have a racial genius for language. Do you realize

The Judge

that even the poorest, most uneducated Mexican uses the subjunctive mood?"

"*Fuegame,*" the Mexican said again, giggling behind his hand.

"Maybe, maybe," the Judge said. "Or better than that, if you don't act sensibly, I might have a look at those records in the courthouse. The ones with your name." He said it pleasantly, and aware that the expression on his face was one of brightness and humor, with his eyes twinkling, yet he wanted a threat in his words, and there was. The Mexican was running again inside.

"How old are you?" the Judge asked suddenly, trusting it was the right question.

Intelligence flicked and vanished in the Mexican's face the way a lizard's tail slips away between sun-baked rocks, and the Judge was left gazing at the place where understanding had been. And slowly, with exquisite precision, the Judge's mind eased open and gave up to him his secrets in the order in which he needed them: the Mexican's age did not match his name. This Mexican's age was decades short of what was needed to match those yellowing, smudged courthouse records. He had "bought his name," as the Mexicans put it, and his papers were forged.

The Judge was home free.

"*I was reminded of the last will and testament of one of the first Spanish conquistadores. 'Before us,' he had written, 'there was no evil, now there is no good.' A moving sentiment, but is it history? The Aztecs could not have been conquered if the majority of the Indians in the Valley of Mexico had not joined Cortez's crew precisely because the Aztec rule had been so cruel; so evil, indeed, that they were willing to follow anyone else in order to overthrow that rule. Our Spanish testator erred in the way we all do—what we do not understand, we always simplify.*"

"Has the Sheriff ever looked at those records of yours in the courthouse?"

There was no more running now inside the Mexican, just the quick blinking of his eyes, the rabbit caught, and waiting.

"You look to me, Baille," the Judge said, "like a man who may have himself some trouble."

The Mexican waited.

"Listen," the Judge said, "I could go on away from here right now without any signature of yours on any papers. I don't need it. I can prove from the records in the courthouse that I don't need it. But I'm not going to do that. I've made up my mind to help you. I know all about you, and you'll have to do what I say. Do you understand?"

"It would be all right if you went away from here now," the Mexican said. "You can do that."

"Don't think it is just altruism on my part," the Judge said. "If I don't get your signature on the papers, it will not look right, because there are people who know your name should be in this case. So if you do not sign, I will have to explain why you did not, and I will have to tell about your records. Do you see? I will have to tell, and then the Sheriff will know about you, and then he would come for you. Understand?"

The Judge set himself to sound absolutely commanding, and it was easy because he had come to that key moment when he knew he was winning and was enjoying his skill at closing a case.

"Now, you go on in there and change your clothes," the Judge said firmly. He knew better than to give the Mexican any time. "I am going to take you with me into town to sign those papers." The Mexican's fast-blinking eyes kept wavering away, glancing off toward the road and the brush around. "Oh, yes," the Judge said, "yes, right now. You go put on something else, something cleaner that you can wear to the courthouse. Go on. Now. And while you're changing, I'll go take a look at your lake."

"Mud pond—that's what I usually call these unimproved water holes when I'm not trying to be nice to the people living near them. Little indentations in the ground they are, no deeper than the hollow in a beggar's palm and filled with thick brownish water evaporating away from the muddy banks. Often one end will go deeper, keeping a permanent water supply, and willows grow up all around it. Any of you noticed these little ponds? Ah, you should. These sites are going to be worth good money one of these days."

The Judge crossed the road and walked alongside it, and the soles of his shoes snapped down the brittle grass that grew and burned and grew again out in the sun beside the road. Once into the shade of the willow trees the grass thickened and made a soft cushion under the Judge's feet. He went straight to the deep part of the pond. As he went he kicked in the reeds and fallen tree limbs for frogs or turtles or any signs of the small animals that exist in the banks near water. Just at the end of the pond there was a little rise of ground. It was not more than three feet high, but in the midst of the violent flatness of the countryside around it seemed higher, and the Judge, coming out from the fringe of willows and putting aside their frail branch tips with the side of his hand, pulled himself up onto it with his short legs and felt he could see a long way, felt he could see for miles. He looked across the pool to the low brush beyond and the dense trees of pale green and gray on the other side. He would have been embarrassed to say how stirred he was by the countryside, or how much beauty he saw in the tangle of mesquite trees growing in a solid cloud on their thin, crooked trunks. He would not have wanted to tell of a game he played, when he was out in the country, of letting his eyes rise only slowly, slowly along the low line of brush and small mesquite, and inch by half-inch go along the solid mass, then slowly lift to the first few broken spaces in between, and moving faster, a little faster and rising again, up and farther along, and going with joy now, joy, up and faster and off over mesquite and willow to the horizon and the dumb unbelievable idiot palm trees grinning like God, he told himself, over the long flat landscape running beneath them all the way to the sea.

"It wasn't easy. I tried just about everything on him. I made three trips out to the school to see the principal, and I made sure each time that Baille saw us together. That preyed on him. He would hang around in the hall pretending to sweep out but watching us. That fool principal spent all the time carrying tales to me against Baille. He told me the Mexican sneaks the lock shut on the boys' washroom once a week or so, and then hangs around in the hall to watch the fun. I was supposed to be shocked at this. Especially shocked because Baille thinks it's funny. The principal is naive. He doesn't understand their humor. More than that, I think it bothers him that I like Baille. He can't understand why I want to help him. At heart, the principal has no feeling for them."

The Judge's attention was caught, by a sound? a smell? and he turned his head and the Mexican was there beside him. The Judge opened his mouth to speak, thinking to ask why the other was in the same clothes and had not changed, when all at once the whole of the Mexican—body, head, shoulders, arms, legs—came leaping into the Judge and jolted him so hard that he hurt all through his body. The two of them fell, not backward and so down the slope of the little hill and into the shallow water as the Judge thought they would and the Mexican intended, but straight onto the muddy lip at the deep edge of the water, just below where the Judge had been standing. For the Judge had been felled absolutely, had had his short legs collapse right under him and had fallen with the Mexican on top of him. They rolled from side to side on the muddy ground, and the willows shaded them some of the time, and the position of sky and lake and trees kept shifting in their line of vision.

All the time the Judge kept grunting and trying to get his breath to say something like: But this is an accident and I accept your apology for stupidly and clumsily and accidentally knocking into me; I understand; while the Mexican pulled at the Judge's head and shoulders trying to haul and shove him farther forward into the water, deep enough to cover his head and face entirely. Reeds at the water's edge snapped beneath the Judge's head, and a rock under his shoulder made him arch his back up in pain as he tried to roll free from the Mexican's hands, which fled from his head and face back to his arms and tugged and pushed at him again, moving him forward once more, farther into the water.

This time the Judge realized what was happening, and focused his eyes finally on the Mexican's face close above his own. The Judge's body jerked rigid and then turned frantic with terror. He grabbed at the Mexican's wrists, uselessly, then tried to get a hold anywhere on the skin that was thin and taut over muscle and bone, and not able to do that, clutched at the worn overalls, but he could not grasp hold of the Mexican in any way. "Knee him in the groin, knee him in the groin," yipped some part of the Judge's mind, delighting him with his own tough knowledge. But his legs thrashed foolishly and uselessly up and down, miles, it seemed, away from the Mexican straddling his chest. The Judge could not even kick the man in the back. The Judge pulled again, and again with no effect, at the Mexican's small hard wrists. With a hiss the Mexican shoved and slid him another few inches into the water and once more tried to submerge the heavy, golden head. There was not enough water, simply not enough water, and in a rage of despair the Mexican grabbed the Judge's head and pressed it deep into the mud. The shallow sludge filled the Judge's left ear and shut one eye, and the nostril on that side was plugged as solidly as by a finger. But the Judge's entire head would not go under. His free eye saw a reed inches in front of his face. It seemed gigantic, the strands that formed it long and beautifully green, and the edges of it the most incredible sharp yellow. The Judge strained toward it, moving with great effort, his head rising out of the mud and water. The Mexican hissed by his ear and got a different grip under the Judge's shoulders and hauled him forward again, deeper into the water. The Judge could feel mud under his shoulders now and dampness down to his waist, and water washed against his neck and up to his ears. With a deep grunt of satisfaction the Mexican pushed the Judge's head down again, hard, and this time the whole head and white face went beneath the water.

It was shocking. The Judge's eyes shut at first, but his ears heard all the sounds water takes in from the air but does not give back to it. He could hear hands thrashing in the water, and the sound of the Mexican's voice cursing. He opened his eyes, and he could see the Mexican, could see everything; it was there, but changed because of the layer of water over his face. The Judge went limp and the Mexican, too ignorant, too eager (*"Poor son of a gun. They're so often like that, defeating themselves by lack of experience or lack of self-control"*), pushed forward too fast, thinking it was over, thinking to finish it, rushing, and so rising up on the Judge's neck too high and getting himself off balance for just that instant (*"Timing has always been one of my greatest courtroom assets, you know"*), so the Judge gave a heave of his powerful stomach and short legs and rolled up and over his own shoulder, tossing the two of them backward, half-somersaulting, and crashing through the reeds and over the muddied lip of the pool and down into the clearer, deeper water. Wet now to hip, to chest, and at any minute over the head possibly, but the Judge was not to know, for the Mexican had turned and flung himself at the shore, crying out for it, lunging back to the bank with the Judge hanging on around his hips while the Mexican grasped and tugged on the reeds, pulling great, sucking chunks of them out of the mud and lunging back again at them and seizing thick sheaves of them in his hands. And all the time the Mexican kept making hoarse, gasping noises, steadily louder, until with a burst of strength he tugged the two of them out of the lake and plunged onto the muddy bank where they fell, crushing the reeds down into the mud.

The Judge propped himself on his knees but kept hard hold of the Mexican as they panted side by side. Streaks of mud curled down the sides of the Judge's face. "Listen," the Judge gasped. "Listen." But he could not get enough air for the words. He was bursting, bursting with joy. He had had a fight. He, the Judge, at his age, had had a fight, like any man, and with a Mexican.

"Listen," the Judge said, holding on to the Mexican's arm just under the shoulder, holding tight, lovingly. "Don't be frightened," the Judge said. "I understand. I am a man, too. I won't bring any charges against you for that. I know how you feel. I won't call the Sheriff. Understand? I know you had to fight."

"Have you ever seen a Mexican cry? A Mexican man, I mean? A grown man? Not the way we do, but with a little 'hee hee hee' noise. Sitting back on his heels with his head pressed against his knees and crying 'hee hee hee,' like that. Just like that."

"See here. Now, see here," the Judge said. "It's going to be all right. It's going to be fine. You can trust me."

The Mexican would not move or lift his head from his knees.

"I'll come out here tomorrow," the Judge said. "At ten. Ten in the morning. And I'll take you to town. And I'll call the principal personally and explain to him that you won't be at work so you won't have any trouble there. You be ready at ten sharp. Understand? Then you can sign those papers. Look, it will be fine. Fine. Don't be scared. Don't . . . don't make noises. Please. Don't. Why listen, listen, you may have . . ." and he stopped. "Saved my life," the Judge wanted to say, but inexcusably he could not remember the verb "to save" in that sense in Spanish. "You may have kept me from drowning," he said. "Saved my life," he remembered, "that's it. You may have saved my life."

The Mexican at least stopped making the noise. The Judge shook his arm in comradely fashion.

"That's right. That's right," the Judge said. "See?"

"No, of course we didn't shake hands. They don't make agreements in that fashion. But by an old, mutually understood joke I became his attorney. Yes, that's it, that's the truth, I was made his counselor by humor, and to be honest, I don't have a better contract, I can swear to that. It was an extraordinary experience; he's an unusual man. All the same, I think I may take up judo on the side if my practice continues in this way."

"Of course you understand now," the Judge said. "Certainly. You probably saved my life, and so I want to help you, too. I'll come out here for you tomorrow at ten. Ten in the morning. You be ready. Hear? You be ready, or I'll have to go get the Sheriff to shoot you. Our joke. Right? Ha ha. Our joke."

In the morning the Judge changed his mind. It seemed to him the best and most courteous thing would be to save the Mexican the trip into town and to the courthouse. Instead, the Judge decided to take his secretary, who could act as notary, and the necessary papers, and go out into the country and let the Mexican sign the papers there. The Judge liked the idea of the gesture. He would meet the Mexican more than halfway. And in any case, the Judge did not know how he and the Mexican, with the closeness that they had between them now, would manage in town, for the town was not ready for that yet.

The Judge went first thing, as he always did, to get his morning newspaper. The newsstand attendant was waiting for him. An obese man, he was squeezed into the narrow doorway of the shop with the Judge's paper held folded and ready.

"You heard?" the attendant asked eagerly. The Judge, as was his custom, dropped a quarter into the brass bowl although the paper cost only ten cents. The attendant kept hold of the paper until he could finish his story. "Haven't you heard? Really? They's a Messgun drowned in the river. Sheriff says it's one you know. Says you know him for sure. I was the second one down to the bridge to see him. I could see him plain as I see you. He was washed up nearest the American side, and he still had a bundle with his things in it tied around his wrist. He was curled up and lying real funny, sort of right on his head and knees, like a little brown snail, and down back of him there was a trail going all the way he'd come out of the river. Everyone wondered where his hat was, but I told him any idiot would know a hat would be the first thing to float on off. Isn't that the truth, Judge? Any idiot ought to know that. But you know something I don't get, how come Messguns don' learn to swim since they keep crossing back and forth in that river all the time? You'd think they'd learn to swim, I say. Now, you take my sister's boy, he's learned to swim good and he's only fourteen. If they'd have learned to swim, them Messguns, none of them would have never drowned."

The Judge stood on the sidewalk with his feet planted square and carefully apart. He had a wide staring look on his face as if an arrow had shot straight through him from back to front going at a great speed and he was looking way off in the distance after it for some vital part of him that was being taken away faster and faster and faster away over the long, flat Texas landscape. Then the Judge gave a sudden, violent jerk, as happens sometimes when falling asleep, or waking.

"So what I say," the attendant said, "is someone ought to teach them to swim. That's what I say."

The Judge turned and began walking away, stamping off with hard steps pounding on the sidewalk.

"Want your paper?" the attendant called after him. "Judge?"

The Judge did not answer. He was getting into his car. He turned it around in the middle of the street and started straight out into the country to the Mexican's home.

He drove the distance in the same way that he always did, at the same carefully restrained rate of speed. There were not even many other cars on the highway, and he got there in the same time that it took him on the quiet Sundays.

The Judge

There was no sign of life from the shack or from the treeless area of dirt around it. The gate hung open, slanting crookedly onto the ground. The Judge turned off the engine of his car.

"Baille!" he yelled at the shack. "Baille!"

The Judge got out and slammed the door hard and began to walk through the sparse grass and the dust that heat and wind had worn to a powder. He walked cautiously, as if at any minute he expected to be struck lame by a stiffening in both knees, an affliction he had felt creeping up on him from a long time past and which he dreaded because he knew that like old rusted locks, it was something no oil or ointment or paid-for expert he might hire was ever going to loosen for him again.

"Baille!" the Judge yelled.

There was no point in standing still before the open gate. The Judge went through it into the yard where he had never been before. He walked toward the corner of the shack around which he was used to seeing the Mexican come. He supposed there must be some sort of door on the other side. When he turned the corner he saw a square black opening in the wall before him. "Baille?" he called again, when he had reached the door, "Baille?" and there being no reply, he lowered his head and plunged into the darkness inside.

There was no one there. The Mexican was gone. And the second shock was the size of the room. For somehow the Judge had always imagined rooms and rooms expanding within the small frame of the shack. In his mind, the Judge had thought of the Mexican waiting for him while sitting in a living room or small reading room, with a kitchen off to his left somewhere and at his back a bedroom. The Judge had placed the Mexican there, sitting comfortably, reading perhaps, or walking around at his ease while he waited for the Judge to come so he could match wits with him again. But there was instead a square of space marked off by gray wooden boards and covered with a tin roof and with the bare ground underfoot. There were not even windows cut in the walls. Threads of light spun themselves down through gaps in the roof, and a block of light fell through the doorway like a hunk of wall collapsed onto the floor.

The Judge's eyes adjusted to the dimness, and he could see every part of the room. Quite obviously the Mexican was gone, gone and had meant to go. He had left a coat the Judge had given him, and a pair of pants the Judge had given him, and two black shoes the Judge had given him. But all the rest was gone except the heavy things he could not carry, a table made of railroad ties and next to it a three-legged stool; an old kerosene stove that was thick with rust; a brass bedstead with no mattress.

A cup, still half filled with coffee, was on the table, and the Judge put his palm against its side. It was cold.

"Damn him," the Judge said. He struck the cup a flat blow, lifting it up through the air to smash into the wall. "Damn, damn, damn him," and the Judge kicked the small three-legged stool. It rolled under the table. The Judge kicked one of the table legs, but the table stood firm on thick square legs. The Judge bent over and caught the edge of the table to upend it, but it would not move. He could not budge it. He tugged again, heaving on it, and when it still stood motionless he bent lower, his head just above its surface, and pulled harder, his mouth strained open with the effort and his face glazing with sweat as he pulled and pulled—and he was seeing through the bright sunlight his car just beyond the gate, and realized he had been seeing it for several seconds before he understood that it was possible, that he had been seeing it with that special clarity of vision given by a peephole, a tiny tear-shaped opening between two warped boards.

And he understood that the Mexican had seen him this way. The Mexican had sat there in the dark at this table and had seen him, the Judge; had watched and waited, all the time looking out through the little hole, and seen the car arrive and the Judge get out of it, and watched it all in a flood of garlic-smelling sweat and terror while his heart leaped and raced all over the place inside his frozen, terrified fraud's pose of stillness.

"Your simple Mexican has a grace of bearing and manner that is hard to believe if you have not seen it. Or experienced it, perhaps, is a better way of putting it. Let me give you an example. I drive up to his house, you see, and of course he hears the car, but first I have to sit and wait. There is to be no rushing. Finally, I get out and walk to the

gate, and sometimes I call out to him. Nothing happens. Some ethnic formality of time has to be satisfied first, some proper amount of respect allowed for. Then he emerges and comes forward to meet me at the gate. But it is always just as I become restless and impatient, yet most receptive, that he appears. He comes when I am most alert, most open to meeting with him. He knows this somehow. Then he comes forward, and every time it is done with pride."

"Damn him." The Judge slammed his palms down on the table so hard his cheeks quivered with the blow. "Damn him for a rotten fraud. Damn him." He leaned forward over the table with his arms braced stiffly straight on it. "Damn him to hell, I swear if I could I'd kill him. . . ."

He stared straight ahead at the empty air, and slowly his body sagged down onto the thick black table. His hands slid across the rough surface to the opposite side so that he was half lying on it, almost embracing the wood, with his heavy stomach pressed against the edge.

"I wonder when he started packing?" the Judge said. "I wonder what he used to make the bundle—a secondhand gunnysack and some old begged-for, handed-down rotten piece of twine?"

The Judge's cheek rested flush against the table. Suddenly he stretched out his tongue and licked across a section of the surface, violently hoping it was thick with germs.

He raised his head, and drawn irresistibly, put his eye to the peephole and looked out again through the bright sunlight that was another dimension of his country, and saw his new blue empty chrome-iced car winking and flashing back at him.

"St. John of the Cross," the Judge said, "as we know perfectly well from the writings of Alonso de la Madre de Dios and the dissertation of the brilliant medievalist Jean Baruzi, made a point of choosing for himself the smallest, meanest, darkest cell in the monastery because he knew that from there, when he looked through the tiny window out over the fields of Spain, he would see visions. Visions."

OHIO UNIVERSITY LIBRARY

Please return this book as soon as you have finished with it. In order to avoid a fine it must be returned by the latest date stamped below.

NON UNIV.

SEP 3 1985

SEP 3 1985

QUARTER LOAN

APR 0 4 1997

JAN 1 6 1997

JUN 1 6 199

MAY 2 7 1997

CF